D0907651

A STATE
OF
SIEGE

Also by Janet Frame

Novels

Daughter Buffalo
Owls Do Cry
Faces in the Water
The Edge of the Alphabet
Scented Gardens for the Blind
The Adaptable Man
Yellow Flowers in the Antipodean Room
Intensive Care
Living in the Maniototo
A State of Siege
The Carpathians

Stories and Sketches

The Lagoon
The Reservoir
Snowman Snowman
Mona Minim and the Smell of the Sun

Poetry

The Pocket Mirror

Autobiography

An Autobiography

Janet Frame

•

A STATE
OF
SIEGE

GEORGE BRAZILLER · NEW YORK

Copyright © 1966 by Janet Frame
Copyright © 1980 by Janet Frame
Reprint

For information, address the publisher:
George Braziller, Inc.
60 Madison Avenue
New York, NY 10010-1682
Library of Congress Catalog Card Number 66-20188

Printed in the United States of America
Designed by Jennie R. Bush
This book was written while the author held the New Zealand Literary Fund
Scholarship in Letters for 1964.

ACKNOWLEDGMENTS

Every effort has been made to credit the holders of copyright of the poetry
and prose selections quoted by the author. We acknowledge the following
permissions:
p. 51, W. H. Auden and Christopher Isherwood, from *The Dog Beneath the
Skin*, copyright 1935 and renewed 1962 by W. H. Auden and Christopher
Isherwood. Reprinted by permission of Random House, Inc., New York.
pp. 190–91, William Kean Seymour, first and fifth verses from "Sheep Bones,"
in *Collected Poems* (1946). Reprinted by the author's kind permission.
p. 212, Hilaire Belloc, from "Tarantella." Reprinted by permission of the publisher, A. D. Peters & Company, London.
p. 239, Albert Camus, from *L'Exil et le Royaume*, © Editions Gallimard,
Paris. Reprinted by permission of the publisher.
pp. 245–46, Sheila Natusch and A. H. Reed Company, from "New Zealand
Rocks" by Sheila Natusch. Reprinted by permission of the author and
publisher.

ISBN: 0-8076-0986-2

To

R.H.C.

A STATE
OF
SIEGE

part one

•

THE
KNOCKING

• 1 •

A SOUTH PACIFIC PARADISE. An island where storms were stormier, rain was rainier, sun was sunnier; where figs, bananas, passion fruit, pawpaws, fijoas, custard apples, guavas, grew and ripened; where the cold pale narcissi opened their buds at the official beginning of winter, and violets bloomed all year; where the only enemies of man, apart from man, were wasps as big as flying tigers, a few mosquitoes breeding a giant island strain, too many colonies of ants; and perhaps, though one does not explain why, the sullen gray mangroves standing in their beds of mud in the tidal inlets facing the mainland.

People from all over the country retired to Karemoana. Others owned or rented baches* there, crowding in summer onto the old

* Beach cottages.—*Ed.*

ferry boats with their holiday gear—including children, goggles, frogmen flippers, fishing rods and reels, bathing suits, gray bach blankets, tinned food, sun umbrellas. The island became a world of guitars, beer, love (free and imprisoned), rejoicing, loneliness, louts and sun. The shopkeepers in the small towns and along the unmade roads forgot their fears of bankruptcy and put out hopefully on the counters, already laden with old stock, a few more weevil-infested packets of walnuts and peanuts, and sea-rusted tins of tomato soup. Then, after summer, when the tourists and holidaymakers had gone, the three hundred permanent residents would reclaim their almost-deserted island, and with the space, sun, rain, silence to grow and ripen as freely as the fruit and vegetables around them, they would nurse their individuality, encouraging the growth of the kind of eccentricity that flourishes best on small islands kept fluid in image by the everpresent sight and sound of the sea.

In relation to the rest of the country, Karemoana and the mainland lying in its latitude were "up north" in a foreign climate with foreign inhabitants whose speech and way of life were American, Australian, Polynesian, certainly far from New Zealand. "Up north" was a place blessed with sunlight, warm winds, subtropical ease; its people were prosperous, confident, free; they thought themselves superior, and perhaps they were, cherishing their geographical "king of the castle" delusion while the oppressed south, the true "down under," struggled for political air and attention. The north lured. The population of the south drifted north as to a new frontier, leaving saddened Borough and City Councils, Tourist Boards, and, in some places, ghost towns. There seemed to be no way of bringing home the deserters, nor of encouraging the new settlers to stay after they had been seduced by the tales of returning holidaymakers and by the ecstatic cries of their frost-, snow-, mist-ridden neighbors:

"It's subtropical! The north is subtropical! They grow *oranges.*"

Members of Parliament preferred not to speak of this climatic rift because it was something they could neither control nor promise to change. Everyone knew that *orange* trees grew up north. The southern retaliation that up north the climate was too dry for the best peaches and apricots that furred the trees and the purses of Central Otago, seemed never quite to have the conviction of northern boasts. Orange trees; orange *blossoms;* the fruit hanging golden, ripening in winter; the soft dark figs bursting at the close of a hot summer; tree tomatoes; Chinese gooseberries. And sun. Months of sun.

And all these blessings without the mainland curse of too many people, their motorcars, motor mowers and transistors, were enjoyed on the islands in the gulf—on Huia, Little Colville, Coromandel, and on Karemoana where Malfred Signal of Matuatangi, South Island, came to retire, not too old at fifty-three to enjoy the comforts of the longed-for separate life in an environment that gave the novel illusion of a world abroad, overseas, in a golden vale of orange trees: a South Pacific paradise.

·2·

MALFRED BURIED HER MOTHER (recently dead, worn out in soul and skin and with the same spotted brown patches on both) and saw her father, thirty years dead, set up in bronze on a lonely headland overlooking Matuatangi, before she made the move north. Her going was a pilgrimage against her nature and her family, especially against her family. The fact that it *was* a pilgrimage gave her the strength to carry out her plans: at fifty-three, or indeed at any age, there are so few opportunities to be a pilgrim.

"But Malfred," everyone said, "your father almost built Matuatangi with his own hands, time, patience and money. And you are your father's daughter."

People had a habit of casting this unanimous verdict without being aware of the sentence it imposed. Malfred, with her sister Lucy (married to a local businessman who one day, in his turn, would have his statue set on a lonely headland, if there were any headlands left that were lonely), her brother Graham (member of a law firm in Christchurch), each had a strong sense of family responsibility. It had seemed that a sense of loyalty alone would persuade at least one member of the family to stay in Matuatangi. Lucy had settled there, happily. But everyone knew, and remarked, that it was Malfred who was her father's daughter; and here was Malfred, born and bred in the town (what blackmail, what self-satisfaction in those words *born and bred*), leaving Matuatangi to live in the foreign North Island! Malfred, who had taught art for so many years at the local High School, who had retired early to care for her sick mother, who yet had found time to help in Corso appeals, to organize W.E.A. lectures in the library hall, to paint and exhibit in the Art Society's rooms, those well-loved, local landscapes and seascapes that were prized for their water-color likeness to the original scenes. Why was Malfred Signal deserting Matuatangi? Who did she think she was— Grandma Moses?

There was a farewell evening organized by the Old Girls' Association with a present bought from contributions made by the Old Girls, the Art Society, the W.E.A.; and Malfred prepared to go north with the good, though wondering, wishes of the people of Matuatangi cast for her in the shape of a pair of silver candlesticks, and with her family's good wishes not as solidly expressed in the shape of good advice, instructions to write, reminders of her age, and of the fact that she was her father's daughter.

"In Matuatangi," Malfred told them, "I can scarcely forget it."

Drinking fountains, seats, gates, foundation stones, trees, all had been named after Francis Henry Signal. He was on the Mayoral roll in the Town Hall, in the records of past Library Committees (Athenaeum and Mechanics Institute) and the Boys' High Honors Board. He had been a legend that Malfred had found hard to reconcile with the slight, shy, brown-eyed man that she knew. He'd climbed mountains, too, named peaks in the Southern Alps, had been mentioned in the country's history; yet Malfred remembered most clearly his gentleness, his long silences, his body that did not seem to have the right shape, for he walked as if one of his legs were shorter than the other, and his head dropped to one side. Malfred had been amused at the Apollo-like image cast of him in the bronze statue: his chin was firm, his head erect, his stance determined, almost regal. The sculptor had shaped him as the conventional Hero, and had got away with it, Malfred supposed, because her father, in life and in death, had been treated as time treats so many heroes: his exploits had been given physical expression.

Malfred knew that the family and the townspeople (who are always more shrewd than is to be admitted) were correct in naming her her father's daughter. She was her father's only child. Where Graham climbed mountains, Lucy knew the names of the native trees, but neither had made mountains or trees as separate dreams inside their mind, as Malfred had done. Malfred knew of the "room two inches behind the eyes"; it was filled almost to overflowing; yet for forty years she had kept it locked. She had not planned that her exploration of it would be a dramatic occasion for herself or others. She kept remembering that when she was a child she had kept a fierce-looking beetle in a match-box, not daring to look at it, and then when one day she found the courage to open the box, she found only a shriveled, dry shell. But the shell had once been such a beautiful amber color that having the beetle dead and gone did not seem important, for it had left behind the memory of its color, of the shell that shone—yellow streaks on dark polished gold and amber. It had seemed incredible to Malfred that the thing, for so long un-looked at, had once been a creature, a pet with a name of its own. Howard. Yes, that was his name: Howard.

Malfred knew that she was on no human terms with the "room two inches behind the eyes," that what lay there, treasure or no treasure, did not belong to her, had not been captured by her and given a name. Perhaps it would never be captured and named. Yet she felt that for the first time in her life she was free to explore that room, and the fact that she was seizing the oppor-tunity to explore branded her more surely than any other action had done as her father's daughter. What her father wanted to do, he had done, in time; he had been patient, persevering; his "One day when I get the chance" had remained a genuine excuse, not the way of life it becomes for so many people, through their own deficiencies or through the sly workings of fate.

Malfred had been interested most of her life in painting. She was not sure that on Karemoana she would be inspired to paint; she wanted, first of all, to observe, to clean a dusty way of look-ing. From her collection of water colors she chose to take north with her, first, a painting of the mouth of the Waitaki in early winter; next, an old mill scene depicting the old mill at Matua-tangi; then, a painting of the lonely headland where her father's statue had been set up. Other paintings she chose were a country

scene on a day of a nor'wester, the old Main Street of Matuatangi with its wool and hide stores, early newspaper offices, rabbitskin factory, new foundry. It was when she was trying to limit her
choice of paintings that she realized (though she had known it
for years, passively) how sentimental, colorless, were the images
she had made of the scenes that were dearest to her; the true
images were in her mind; she could stare at the mouth of the
Waitaki in early winter without having to burden herself with a
pile of dusty canvases that would remind her less of the scenes
depicted than of the years spent "teaching" art, pouncing on the
faulty "shadowers," trying to instill the "sense of proportion"
that in her probationary years meant persuading schoolgirls to
"match" the sides of shovels and vases, to make distant mountains distant, near faces near; but which meant to her now an
attempt to rearrange her own "view," set against the measuring
standards not of the eye but of the "room two inches behind the
eyes."

·3·

"IT'S NOT AS IF you're young, Mally. Do you really think you can tear yourself away to go to this island? You've lived in Matuatangi for so long!"

"What would mother think? Did you ever tell her of your plans?"

"Karemoana has only rain water, no sewers."

"Up north! Are you sure you'll like it up north?"

"It's a long way to come south for visits. Do you know what the journey's like?"

"And it's a long way for us to come north to see you."

"The north is vulgar. It takes the biggest bite of everything."

"The south nibbles discreetly. *And* thirty chews to a swallow!"

"You can hear the north eating. Its table manners are bad."

"The south is old-fashioned enough to still use a tablecloth, to put *pepper and salt* on the breakfast table."

"It's hot up north, Mally. The kind of heat that you wouldn't like, at your age. Humidity."

"There's no snow."

"No rivers to speak of."

"And you'd never guess what, in all good faith, they give the name *mountain* to!"

"You'll be a stranger in a foreign land. At your age it's harder to become acclimatized."

"And what of this bach you've bought? What is it, beside our old family home that you're selling, where the three of us grew up and Dad and Mother died?"

"What about your friends, your painting, the Old Girls' Association, the Art Society?"

"I'll allow all your arguments," Malfred said good-humoredly.

"I've an answer to everyone. Not what about the weather, the distance, the isolation, the family, the town, friends, societies, my age. Just— *What about me?*"

They were disconcerted. They had supposed, they said, they had supposed. When they looked again at their sister, at her coarse gray hair wound in plaits, her oval face with its high cheekbones already patched with the pigmentation of age and rising blood pressure, her gray eyes, her full yet primly posed lips, and her body in its autumn-tinted cardigan and skirt, they saw for an instant not the incipient signs usual in a woman past fifty, not the hints of the walking last will and testament, with legacies neatly disposed, but a flame that there was no accounting for, burning steadily at its own pace because it had been lit from within. They did not try to identify or discuss it. Instead, Lucy, so dreamy, untidy and rich, said, "Mally, do come to see the central heating in our new greenhouse, and all the beautiful plants Roland has bought." While Graham said, "When you're passing through Christchurch, Mally, what about spending a couple of days with Fernie and me?"

On her last day in Matuatangi Malfred went with Lucy to visit the family grave in the cemetery. Lucy cleaned the winged angel with a small bottle of detergent she had bought for the purpose, while her small snowy-haired son, Oliver, made daisy chains, with Mally's help, though Malfred was disappointed that he did not see "something special" in the daisy chains. If she'd had children of her own, she thought . . .

She replaced the cleaned glass bell over the pale stiff artificial flowers, forked the chickweed (how lank and tall it grew, twice the size of chickweed on ordinary soil!) and the sow thistle from the borders, then, with their sense of duty and their conscience put to sleep in the warm spring air they unraveled Oliver from his daisies and went back to the car. Lucy then drove to the cape for Malfred to have a last glimpse for many months, perhaps years, of their father's statue.

"Though why we should bother to drive up here, I don't know," Lucy said. "Unless it's for the view. It's too bad that just when they decide to put Dad up here everyone discovers there's a View. The place has been overgrown with weeds for years."

"Nobody came here in the old days," Malfred said. "Lovers, maybe. And old men taking a stroll from the Old Man's Home.

Don't you think Dad would die of horror if he woke to find himself here, now, with this restaurant beside him?"

"It makes me wonder if you're quite sure your island up north, Karemoana, will be the unspoilt paradise you believe it to be."

"I don't expect a paradise."

Why could no one seem to understand? A sense of peace came to Malfred as she realized the lack of bitterness in her question. Indeed, she suspected that she was asking it only out of deference to herself when young, when understanding had seemed as scarce as ownership of a royal kingdom. She felt, too, that the attempts of Lucy and Graham and others to persuade her to stay in the South Island were not based on genuine concern, as if she had been young and in need of care and advice. The objections to her going north were routine objections. Lucy and Roland would miss her, and she would miss them, and little Oliver. She would miss Graham and Fernie, too, and their aloof, grown-up family. And then there would be no more Monday evenings at the Art Society, Ladies a Plate*—all plates because there were all ladies! Your mountains, my lake, her beach in summer. The Old Girls' Association. Yes, Miss Cartright; no, Miss Cartright; more tea, Miss Jefferson? But you don't take sugar, Miss Humphrey!

Then home, and mother. The blue tubes of lanolin in rows and rows on the shelf in the bathroom. Also in the bathroom, the special equipment for the sick, as if the journey to death were a journey into space, with invalids and astronauts practiced travelers in their lonely new environment. Who knows, Malfred thought, that mother at her death did not catch a glimpse of eternity and cry out from the small shriveled capsule that was her final home, "What a beautiful view!" And how jealous her

* Expression meaning "Ladies bring a plate."—*Ed.*

mother had been of the equipment—the bed cradle, the commode, the bed pan; the liniments, pills, injections! Day after day she used to lie in the bed in the front room, calm, but in pain, engaged in a form of stocktaking that would not have pleased the earnest vicar whose mind, naturally or through training, turned to the counting of blessings only; old Mrs. Mary Signal lay counting her medicines, like a grocer stocktaking his wares.

All her life Malfred had felt as if she had been bound in someone else's dream, as she had read that some Eastern children had their limbs bound to set them in the shape desired by their parents and by tradition. In her dream she had painted lakes, boats, mountains, children, cats, dogs; and there had been no consciousness that her arms were asleep, nor any feeling of need to wake them from their approved dreaming. When her mother died, the realization and shock of her freedom gave Malfred a desire to destroy, to strike out, in the spasm resulting from her suddenly cured paralysis. Then she was calm and watchful.

She remembered that she went to the room that had been her father's study, and there she forgot to be calm. She burst into tears that tasted of salt and chalk, the chalk that she had swallowed and sniffed and sprayed out in a poisonous spray of wandering lines during all the years she had "taught" art.

Mother's illness has been a strain, she told herself. I never knew that anyone could settle so happily into dying. Why should she have found it such an enjoyable experience?

At the time of her mother's death, Graham and Fernie had come to stay. There were other relatives, too, from Nelson and Wellington: her mother's youngest brother and his wife and their grown-up son. All tiptoed to the sickroom and peered in possessively at old Mrs. Signal. Malfred noticed that only she had referred to it as the "sickroom," as if her continued association with the dying had shown death in its truly old-fashioned light.

"Mother likes flowers in the *sickroom*," she had said. She was aware, now, that she had spoken in a gloating manner.

Graham, as the man of the family, had seen to the practical arrangements that are part of dying and being disposed of, particularly of being disposed of. They dismissed Malfred as "overwrought" when she said, half-joking (to her surprise, too, for she had not thought she would joke in this way), "Wouldn't it be easier to bury her in the garden?"

She had realized her mistake at once in saying that. She had long grown used to the fact that when a woman without family ties of husband and children makes any reference to or joke about the mysteries of the closed human family, whether about birth, marriage, death or disposal, she is immediately subdued by the argument that only those who have experienced such total mysteries have the right to comment on them.

Bury mother in the garden indeed!

"Now if I said that about any of *mine*," Fernie began, then she stopped. Malfred was looking at her with a glance that said clearly, "Mother was not *mine*."

Well they could have her, Malfred thought, aware of rising hysteria. They could have her. *She* didn't want her any more, *she* didn't want her supermarket of medicines. But it hadn't always been that way. Her mother had been gentle, she had seen things clearly, until her last illness.

Perhaps, Malfred thought, I did look upon her as my possession. Though I've been saying all my life that I can do without anyone, I must have someone. I've always needed someone, even if it's only for the snobbish reason of keeping up with the

Joneses. My he, she or it can't be forever away on holiday or in the country or the city or at sea or unborn or lost or dead. How I hated mother! She was enclosed, not in a space capsule in preparation for a voyage that would give her a wonderful view of the stars, of eternity, but in one of those medical capsules the skin of which is dissolved, digested, by those who swallow them. I've seen hot water poured on those capsules; they are dark blue; they twist, they melt.

Mother walked with me one day in spring when the cherry blossom was out in the Avenue, and she turned to me and said, "Matuatangi with its cherry blossom is the prettiest town in the South Island. Pretty, but full of gossips."

The night her mother died Malfred dreamed that she walked in a room carpeted with tubes of lanolin with their caps dislodged so that the stuff squirmed in a greasy mess over her best shoes; then the blue tubes of lanolin changed to tubes of oil paint. Malfred wound her hair in its gray plait and straightened her cardigan. She smiled in her sleep. "I'm painting mother," she said. But in the morning when she woke she did not remember her dream and so could not use it, as people like to use dreams, as an omen of her future. Instead, she woke with a nasty taste in her mouth, and a bad breath that could not be masked, and in her eyes and on her cheeks were muddy tears left by the tide of death that had come in, taken what it wanted, then gone out leaving all grief stranded with not even a solitary, pink sea anemone flowering in the rock pool.

· 4 ·

SHE KNEW, BUT HAD not realized, the peace that came from staying year after year in the same place. She did not want to see herself as a timid woman, past middle age, alone, setting out on a tiring, perhaps a frightening journey to a new home in a part of the country that was strange to her. She could not get out of her head the idea of orange trees. Other people seemed impressed by them, too.

"Up north?" they would say. "Orange trees grow up north. Oranges, figs and lemons. But *oranges*."

Yet when the Limited for the north drew in at Matuatangi station and the passengers, steamed warm, prosperous, assured, crowded onto the platform, staring with their condescending

North Island eyes at the obvious attempt that had been made to jazz up the refreshment room, to "centralize" sales by offering magazines side by side with buns, and not only buns—hamburgers, a crescent of burnt onion stuck to a slice of freckled Belgium—then Malfred knew she was afraid, or perhaps more excited than afraid, though the excitement was anchored at intervals (like a magic carpet pelted and weighed down with heavy stones) by the practical worries: would her luggage get there safely, her books, her painting materials, the few personal treasures she had chosen to take with her? Why were her suitcases so heavy when they had not seemed so at home? Would the crossing be rough? Would she have access to the ventilator in the cabin? And the day in Wellington, how would she spend it? Trying to escape from relatives, walking up and down Willis Street in the everlasting misty rain? Looking in Whitcombes, going to the Houses of Parliament, visiting an art gallery to see the fruits that she and her contemporaries had tried to ripen but had succeeded more often in withering? She remembered taking a class from the High School to Wellington for the Centennial Exhibition. The crossing was rough; most of the girls were sick. They had spent the night in barrack-like conditions in a local school, and the day wandering drearily around the Educational Court, hardly able to wait for their ration of "free" time before they rushed to the Ghost Train, the Big Wheel, the Bearded Lady, and the Fire-Eating Magician. And when they returned to Matuatangi their paintings, "My Trip to Wellington," "The Exhibition," "The Cable Car," "A Wellington Street Scene," had been so uninspired, so lacking in color and originality, that it seemed as if the visit, far from giving the girls a spurt of mental growth, had had the effect of an application of D.D.T. Malfred knew that when she had said in despair, "What did you really *see* in Wellington, girls?" the disappointment had been directed chiefly at herself: what had *she* seen? The same dull uninspired images that yet had not seemed dull and uninspired, for they had been the result of the ingrained habit of dutiful looking, of seeing what was there, and what others agreed was there, which was a less arduous and hazardous way of coming to terms with the shapes and colors of everything, including wet and windy Wellington during Exhibition Week, than other ways of looking.

Malfred sighed. Who had put lead sinkers in her suitcases? She felt, suddenly, too middle-aged, tired, dignified, to explore her past. It was only the night her mother was dying that she realized what she had missed seeing by her dutiful habit of looking. And now she knew that she could not forget the sight of her mother's skin as she lay dying: its pallor, the marks—like faint blue lines of carbon—at the base of her neck where her pulse flicked irregularly like a trapped midge under a thin yellow leaf. Had the others seen what she had seen? Malfred wondered.

The Waitaki Bridge. The clumps of willows, the tongue-shaped places where the water suddenly stretched to fit and flow over the round, white, smooth stones; the glitter of the sun on the water—how often she had painted the Waitaki, milky, muddy, clear, green, running like sap out of the gashed sides of the mountains!

The train knocked, jolted over the worn bridge, moving slowly, carefully, above the swirling water; then there were the still pools surrounded by flood and foam making a circle of quietness around an upthrust dead willow with trapped grasses clinging like fur to its outstretched gray branches; then, halfway over the bridge, the feeling of isolation. Beyond the Waitaki the land was foreign. Oh yes, there were plains, magpies, gum trees, the far hem of the Alps, dark blue or white; the grass thin, gold; the small stations—Commercial Hotel, Railway Hotel—that would not go away or change over so many years; the sad slicing of the tall windmill—striped warnings at the deserted level crossings; dark blue, curved cars passing swiftly, parallel to the train, flying from city to city, dense, packed with color, beside the thinly dispersed stalks of yellow grass. Where was the foreignness in these scenes that Malfred had known most of her life in Otago and Southland?

Watching intently, trying to seize the New View, Malfred identified the strangeness. She had known it before. She'd stayed with Graham and Fernie in Christchurch while she attended Art Exhibitions and Refresher Courses there. She'd crossed the Waitaki, going north, many times. She'd painted the plains, from sight and from memory, and people had admired her paintings. Yet she knew, now, that in none of her paintings had she ever described the way in which the plains submitted, a world without walls save for the western, dark blue rim of distance, to the invasion of light and air and snow-colored water. The nor'wester came like a living thing with choking dust-filled breath, on and on, past the windbreaks of firs and gum trees, the red-roofed homesteads, to roam unchallenged across the plains. The light fell unconcealed in a harsh flood from the sky to merge, softening, with the miles of yellow grass and wheat, then to rise suspended above the grass in a soft haze that beckoned distance, mountain winds, and the current of loneliness that flowed from the hearts of those who sat in the Limited, the afternoon Boat Train from Invercargill, going north, and leaned their elbows against the soot-spattered window, and looked out at the sheep, the black cattle, the fir trees and the gum trees, the fences, the gates, and wept for the millions of drooping grass-heads, barley, wheat, rye and common couch that were not people. Where were the people to look on the scene and know its meaning? To look north, south, east and west? Malfred knew the heaviness of heart that always overcame her, crossing the plains. Such a burden of seeing was put upon each traveler, more than could be borne. But not all were aware of it—they dozed, read, ate, talked, smoked, then dozed, though some could not help saying aloud, as if it were the most articulate national prayer that would put the situation right with Him or Those who were in a position to take care of such things, "It's a great country all right, a great country."

·5·

THE LIGHT ON BOARD the ferry was warm, golden brown, reflected in the newly painted walls. The white coats of the stewards divided the light into squares. As soon as Malfred emerged from the white-hooded gangway onto the ferry (Gangway A; the passengers using it walked with conscious pride in the superiority of A over B), she knew the painting she would make of the scene. It would be like no other painting she had made. It would be part of her New View. Perhaps it would not be admired by those who were pleased to recognize in her work the place where they had picnicked last summer, the beach or river they had bathed in, the corner or camp where they'd pitched their tent, the gorge they'd driven through. The painting, *On Board the Ferry,* would be a series of golden brown and white squares. That was all a steward was, Malfred thought with sudden tiredness and an impatience that surprised her—a white square; no, a rectangle; and some wore black. And surely it's too late, she thought, for me to paint the New View. I'll have to be content with seeing, seeing, and clarifying in my head what I have seen. Yet . . .

Bells rang; people laughed, talked. The brass rails shone. Malfred went at once to bed, in the bottom bunk. The top bunk stayed unslept in. No one came with bags and cases and the sharp smell of perfume or powder, claiming too much room; wanting the ventilator turned the other way, the light on or off or on. Malfred turned the ventilator towards the wall and fell asleep with the roaring noise in her ears; blood or sea; and in the middle of the night, waking for ten seconds only, merged with sleep, feeling the warm brown smell of the boat's going, the steady busy purpose (the towel rail gleamed; Malfred felt safe to know that the slim piece of shipping company soap lay in its hollow in the rim of the washbasin), she thought, "I'm a fool, at my age, to go north to live. To an island, too. I never dreamed I was so tired. I hope my checked luggage tickets are safe."

Then she fell asleep again, and in the morning, after a cup of tea and a biscuit, she joined the throng of passengers outside her door, tripping over piled luggage, caught, against her will, in the panic that had seized everyone, the fear that the ferry would berth and they would not be first, second, or third ashore, that somehow they would be left behind. Ashamed, but unable to help herself, Malfred took her turn at elbowing, propelling herself to a place near the gangway. It's not as if, she thought wonderingly, there's a train to catch. Like at Lyttleton. What has come over us? Then, remembering, though she had known it all the time, that she did not really want to be first, second or third ashore, she relaxed, sat on her suitcase, deliberately apart from the crowd, and painted in her mind her New View of them. It was not flattering. Their hands were hooks. Some had gashed faces. All stood against a background of squares and rectangles of golden brown and white light.

In Wellington, after a morning of walking in wet mist, choosing sandwiches from beneath a bell-jar like that which encloses everlasting flowers, *immortelles;* drinking coffee, walking by the crane-infested waterfront, seeing the hills mile-up, ton-up in their green leather bush, Malfred chose to spend the afternoon (after a visit to the Soldier's Memorial Rest Rooms, Women Only, Mothers' Room, Bottles Heated) in the Public Gallery of the House of Representatives that proved to be no less memorial and maternal than the Rest Rooms, for there, following the example of the Minister of Defense and others not known to her, she fell asleep.

Waking, when the House rose at half past five, she felt more interest than shame. She set herself, her story, in the confined space of a coffin prose: fifty-three, alone, sighted, seeing, slept through Defense Legislation.

·6·

THEN FOLLOWED THE DIMLY lit, meat-pie journey to Auckland, in a shelf-like top bunk when she had especially asked for a bottom bunk, but no one cared or explained or apologized. Breath soot-high; voices when the train stopped, voices sharp and clear as footsteps walking the platform of the station; steam clouding like cottonwool; heavy-eyed sleep, eyelids sealed with specks of soot. Then early morning, cold clothes with too many arm and feet holes, a fawn railway-colored, blanket-colored biscuit; tea; a newspaper. And then, at the end of the jolting, heaving journey over railway lines that had surely been cut on the bias, a slow, measured halting, and in the scatter of people waiting, promising cars and warm homes, crying welcome from Auckland Station, not a soul that knew or was known by Malfred. Tired, faintly anxious, yet lighthearted, anonymous, she went, showing more confidence than she felt, to the Checked Luggage Department to be re-united with her six suitcases that seemed naked, without rope or strap protection, beside the others, heavily corded and banded, waiting to be claimed. Venice, Paris, Southampton. Initial letters chalked on the sides proved that some lucky persons had "traveled," had "passed the Customs." The few pieces of furniture and household goods that Malfred had taken from her old home were now, she hoped, waiting for her at Denby and Soames, Haulage Contractors, Karemoana. She had their telephone number—had she? Yes. The creased, brown, shot-silk torn lining of her handbag revealed not only her receipt from Denby and Soames but her own age and generation, her conformity, the desire for convenience that had made a handbag necessary in her life. Handbag, gloves, shoes to match. Hat to town in the afternoons or on Fridays.

Handbag, gloves, shoes to match. The creed, so faithfully learned and followed, brought no response now. Sensing the Crisis, the Moment, Malfred, standing at the Checked Luggage Department, prayed to the God whom she believed in that her castoff social creed might be replaced not by one as equally time-consuming and shallow (she recognized the danger here) but by one that could stand without incongruity side by side with new seeing; one that would take for its practice symbols more durable, more worthy, than handbag, gloves, shoes to match.

In her hotel room at the top of Queen Street, booked for one day and night because the family had persuaded her she would need "time to recover from the dreadful North Island train journey," Malfred sat alone, depressed, knowing that the full

27

agony of metamorphosis lay in its being a gradual process recorded by a personal time which translated the mythical "overnight" almost into the length of years between birth and death;
knowing that Upper Queen Street, Auckland, was not a very
favorable place to come to such a conclusion. Looking from her
window onto the street, she counted the bones of new buildings,
more numerous, cared for and modern than the bones of many of
the people who passed beneath them. She remembered that the
season was spring, but it was not the cool, clear, golden, southern
spring; it was a still day with the sky full of clouds and the air
strangely warm, as if suffering from a low fever that communi-
cated itself to the passers-by who looked around and up and
down, in a kind of sweating anxiety; perhaps, walking under the
half-made buildings, they interpreted the web of scaffolding in
its more sinister meaning. Only the workmen seemed happy.
One, a big man wearing a checked shirt, saw Malfred and waved
at her; definitely a wave. Malfred waved back with a sudden
jettisoning of good will and energy. From her high window she
seemed like someone in a plane who empties all fuel and cargo,
still hoping against hope that the plane is not doomed to crash.

Then she shut the window, crossed to the wardrobe, and
looked at herself in the long mirror.

"A rectangular package," she said. "I'm still not too old to
wonder what my body is for, why it has stayed with me through
thick and thin; a spare part kept to replace nothing. Yet I've not
suffered greatly from it, as some women may."

(Yes, Miss Henderson; no, Miss Wallace; do you take sugar
and milk, Miss Ford?)

All was well. Solitude; far from the vulgar crowd; seeing,

analyzing the New View; perhaps painting it. Ideal retirement lay waiting at Karemoana.

(Yes, Miss Henderson; no, Miss Wallace, do you take milk and sugar, Miss Ford?)

Malfred felt homesick, suddenly, for the Old Girls' Tea, for the Ex-Staff-Members' Gatherings, the picnic to Trotter's Gorge, or the Willows.

And now the flat silver tongue of the Waitaki would be lying lapped by the incoming tide. She could taste the snow in the water.

"The land is all I need," she said to herself. "I'll stare at it, I'll see it. I'll paint it as I see it. I understand why my father spent so much time beyond the Southern Lakes, in the Southern Alps. We are so few in this country. It is the land that is our neighbor, the rivers, the sea, the bush that we have loved as ourselves. My duty (she recognized in herself the characteristic need, developed and maintained through the years, to move from duty to duty) is to *see,* perhaps to have the energy, the courage, to paint what I see, and since my island is sparsely populated there'll be no intrusion of people into my scenes. Fifty-three is a ripe enough age to put aside entanglements with the human family.

"Great thoughts in a hotel room," she mocked, standing respectfully aside while one of the floating band of housemaids, suiting her movement to her species, came to clean the mirror above the washbasin and the glass top of the dressing table, explaining as she did so that the housekeeper was a bitch.

Malfred was shocked.

"Surely not!"

The housemaid looked at her, including her. "They're all bitches," she said.

Sensing the need for proportion and discipline, Malfred was about to adopt her schoolteacher manner, to try to get the girl to "think through" the problem, to compare known bitch with unknown-but-rumored bitch, to make a standard of bitchery by which detached judgment could be made; but it was no use. Dismayed, she knew that she was indeed "one of them." Take out your water colors, girls. Mind your mixing. Remember the color wheel. Take out your pencils, your drawing book D. Watch your shading.

"All alike," the girl said. This time, subdued, Malfred agreed with her.

"Though what," the girl said scathingly, "you should know about it is a mystery. You're a *guest*."

Malfred rested thankfully on her privilege, trying to diminish the importance of being a guest by explaining that she didn't usually stay in hotels, that she had come up north to stay, to live.

"Retire? They all come north. For the climate."

The girl relaxed into a summer smile. "My boyfriend has a fourteen-foot runabout."

"Oh?"

It was no use again, she had lost touch, she didn't approve of runabouts, anyway, and she couldn't pretend to. She was fifty-three, she wanted a quiet life in which to paint what she had seen. But what had she seen? She had forgotten, already she had forgotten; she was tired, the room "two inches behind the eyes" beckoned less than the hotel bed, mercifully motionless after the railway sleeper.

That night, when Malfred at last went to bed, she gave way to the regrets that haunted her, and lay in misery; but before she slept she was able to realize again, with clarity, that her move north had been, for her, the only possible means of survival. She wondered, though, if she were not relying too much on the island, on Karemoana, to provide all that she felt to be missing from her life.

The island. Karemoana. Small are islands, forever fluid in image, seen once only, escaping, a rabbit thumping the sea.

·7·

A MAN WITH A LONG scroll under his arm and a desire, expressed to his companion, to lunch on pinky bars and chocolate fish, sat near Malfred on the ferry. He was going across to survey properties, he said. His friend, a sculptor, had been hired to make garden statues. Things were booming on Karemoana. Sections were being cleared, sold, built on. A hydrofoil, ordered from Italy, would be arriving any day, would cut down the traveling time by two thirds.

"You're in the swim, coming to Karemoana," the man said, turning to Malfred, who had not spoken to him, had told him nothing of herself. She struggled between pride and horror at being "in the swim." She marveled that the tide of a flow she had not cared for or indeed acknowledged should sweep her, a stray twig, in its path.

She was sitting in the narrow passageway outside the cabin, so that she could have the wind in her face, and see the landmarks of the harbor and the gulf. Malfred was always aware of her need for fresh air. Sometimes she paused, sadly, to recognize that with increasing age and the need to hold fast to personal character- istics lest they be buried, leaving nothing particular or special to highlight the label *Malfred Signal*, what had once been a casual, hygienic preference for "fresh air" had become an obsession, an addiction. She had become the kind of person who opens win- dows on entering buses and rooms and cabins, and when there is no window to open, who adjusts ventilators, switches on fans. She knew that, publicly, she had made the first move towards being known as a "crank."

Her cheeks glowing with the keen wind, she watched the sea. She wondered dreamily, seeing a beer bottle float by, if there were a message inside it, and if there were, what were the con- tents of the message. She listened to the conversation about her. It dealt mostly with island topics, events, places, people that were strange to her. Sometimes a young boy and girl passed, jeaned and jerseyed (she pressed her knees against the seat to let them pass), and the boy would have a radio commercial or a soap opera sounding out of his pocket from the transistor that had become, without replacing others tried and tested by centuries, the new fashionable male member. Malfred almost felt young again, but she knew that the feeling was both forced and false, for the distance between her and the young boy and girl was too great, and she was honest enough to realize this, and not con- demn herself for it, not conceal the distance with a heartiness that was its own shame and admission, more clear than any normal hostility. The stepping stones were gone forever. The river flowed deeper, wider, in full flood.

Malfred gasped suddenly with the pain of homesickness. Were there rivers, *real* rivers, ice green, snow-fed, on Karemoana?

A ridiculous question. She knew the answer. She opened her handbag and took out the photos of the bach she had bought. Graham and Fernie, Lucy and Roland had accused her of unbusinesslike buying "on spec." She had been more careful, she insisted, than if she had inspected the place herself. The photos were explicit, the Auckland solicitor had investigated the title with a thoroughness that earned him his high fee; he had studied the planning arrangements for the district, the condition of the property in rain and sun. The only detail he had neglected to give—at the time it had not seemed important to Malfred, but now, though she hated to admit it, she felt that it mattered almost more than anything else—had been the number and nearness of her neighbors. Why, she told herself, when I'm deliberately escaping from people, do I care so much who my neighbors might be? I don't care, I don't care. The island, the scenery, will be my intimate companion; it is the only formula for living fully in an underpopulated country.

And why, at my age, do I suddenly need a formula?

It will take strength to live my life; half my strength has been lost in the process of uprooting myself.

The berthing of the ferry shook her from her contemplative priggishness. Take care, she told herself. Take care. She smiled at the young handsome policeman who helped her down the gangway.

"It is," she said, when he remarked that it was a fine day for an outing to Karemoana.

But as she walked to the waiting taxi she knew that she'd been surprised, dismayed, to see only the wharf, crowding hills, and no sign of a township. The waiting air of the people on the wharf had a dreariness about it, as if the people had waited too long, for something or someone else, not for the ferry. Malfred could not help thinking of all the small islands she had known or read about, that had been used through the centuries to confine the vicious, the unloved, the diseased. The natural exiling power of islands had never been forgotten, and never would be, as long as man had the desperate need to put out of his sight the living embodiment of those things in himself that he most hated and feared. Malfred smiled bleakly as she climbed into the taxi. There seemed, now, to be so little difference between voluntary and involuntary exile. Why had she imagined they were not one and the same act, with the responsibility alone apportioned differently? And did not everyone know, though few admitted, that the needle of responsibility quivered and pointed, following only the unstable direction of the human temperament?

"You've bought the bach on the hill?"

"Why, yes!"

"Nice place. The owner died about six months ago. Elderly woman—well, maybe not elderly—about your age. Retired. You retired?"

Malfred hesitated. "Yes."

"You know about the woman who lived there before you?"

"No!"

"Nothing to know, really. Not really. You'll be right as rain. Here's the place. Bang on the hill. Best view for miles."

Malfred found that the other passengers in the taxi (to her surprise there *had been* other passengers, the driver packing them in until there was no more room), were staring at her.

"The island looks to be a beautiful place," she said fatuously, throwing approval like silver coins into their eyes and their mouths until they seemed satisfied; but they still stared; in horror.

"I'm sure I'm going to like living here."

She tried not to show surprise at the taxi fare, and not to calculate the profit the driver would be making with his load of seven passengers. Instead she asked, with the deferential smile that she imagined was appropriate for a new inhabitant, "Is there a phone box near? To see about my luggage, you know."

The driver directed her to a phone box at the end of the street.

She waited until the taxi with its staring passengers had gone, then, delaying the moment when she would walk into her new home, she went to the phone box. She noticed as she dialed Denby and Soames that the opaque panes of glass in the phone box were all smashed, in radiating star patterns that preserved the shock of their impact with stones, fists? Or tension within the box itself?

Thank God, she said to herself, as the representative of Denby and Soames spoke to her. Then suddenly his voice faded, there was a regular clicking sound, and the operator said, "Hold the line, please."

"What's wrong?" Malfred asked.

"The usual. Some fool in Auckland. It's *their* side that's always to blame." The operator spoke vindictively.

Then Malfred heard again the voice of the representative of

Denby and Soames. It came, like a prophet's voice to her ear, telling her that all was well, her luggage, yes, yes, the correct number of pieces, was on its way, had probably arrived already and would be delivered that afternoon; furniture, furnishings, suitcases.

Lighthearted, Malfred walked back along the high road. She had not realized the depth of her anxiety, her fear that her "things" had not arrived.

She climbed the steps cut in the grassy path to the white-painted bach on the hill. Putting down her one suitcase she opened her handbag, withdrew the big old-fashioned key on its length of string, fitted it into the lock, turned it, and pushed open the back door.

·8·

THE HOUSE HAD A sitting room with an alcove bedroom, a small separate bedroom, a kitchen, a bathroom, a small indoor lavatory of which the bowl was a rusted oil drum cut down to half-size. There was a shed outside where a broken table, pedestal, other unused furniture, and gardening tools were stored. The small amount of furniture inside the house ("part-furnished" had been the agent's description) was neglected and, Malfred sensed, immediately hostile, presenting edges and corners in direct attack on her shins, knees, hips, ankles. Her first thought was to arrange somewhere to work, or if not to work, to sit and stare, then somewhere to sleep. She chose the small room for both operations. Windows in two walls gave her the light she needed for

38

painting while the narrow single bed, fitted neatly against one inner wall, seemed a private, ideal place for sleeping. Yet, she could prepare for neither work nor sleep until the carriers came with her luggage. She decided to walk to the shop near the telephone box to buy food and other provisions and as she walked along the high road looking down at the sea that glinted silver, gently looping wave on wave, she felt a spontaneous overwhelming love for her surroundings—the sea, the sky, the bush and shrub in the valleys; and she was not ashamed of her love, for she knew the first condition of loving, that there must be an object. Was it too great a loss that the object within sight and reach was not a human creature?

Her body felt at rest. Her skin, replaced from time to time unnoticed by her or by any other person, had at last settled into her body, creased itself against her bones and flesh as if to say, Here's home. It was no small comfort, feeling oneself wanted by one's own skin. The hope that sea, sky, bush would in a similar way surge closer to express a need, however indefinite, had never been more than a fanciful hope, immediately dismissed as one of the more pitiful, regrettable emotions that accompany loneliness. Malfred had long ago found her own solution to the problem of being a single woman. It was the kind of problem that, she found, occupied the minds of others more than her own. Other people simply wanted to know, again and again, how she "managed." They looked out from their cosy cave-like homes (blood under their fingernails where they had shared the flesh of the killed beast, their mouths stocked with imported and exported kisses tottering in moist balance on their tongues) and, their human curiosity surmounting even their preoccupation with mutual need and growth and adaptation, they asked, or if they did not ask they wondered silently, how the people walking alone from birth to death "managed."

Malfred would have liked to retort that living was simply, undramatically, an allotted state of continually having to manage, whether the object was one's body or one's budget or (more important to Malfred now) one's clarity of seeing. The only fact that she felt she could not influence after many years' experience in diverse "management" was her body's being, aging, dying. She had at first imagined that her sudden change of vision, the release of material from her room "two inches behind the eyes" had been a sudden gift of body chemistry. She knew now that it was a cunning means of escaping from inevitable change by taking the responsibility of the change upon herself. Not I am dying, but I die; not I am born, but I bear. Not I am seen, am seen to be a middle-aged, retired teacher of Art, of no great ability or ambition, with usual human needs, with my mother, the tree in the garden that blocked my view, that I cared for, pruned, admired, picked the fading blossoms, now dead, leaving the world exposed in its view before me; not I am seen, but I see, I see. The habit of passive living, of submitting dutifully to the impositions of each day, has turned upon itself.

I think now that I, too, snarl at morning. There is blood beneath my fingernails, too, as I tear the flesh of the killed beast.

Long explanations were needed. Malfred no longer made them against the background of a dying woman and tubes of lanolin. I'm free, I'm free at last, she thought, as getting by, like all human beings, with the necessary self-deception, she entered the prison "two inches behind the eyes."

She made coffee, instant, that left a gray stain inside the cup.

She rested on the alcove bed. And when the carrier came at half past three she received her luggage and furniture calmly as if they were house guests, though once again the uneasy longing for the South Island came over her when the carrier referred to the season.

"Nice spring day!"

Spring?

She could have wept to seek the definition in the vague warm air flowing through the opened front and back door of her new home. The front door looked out on the sea, at the gulf and its islands. In the valley, the gorse, the white manuka flowers were in bloom; it was no use taking their appearance as a seasonal sign. Malfred knew as she looked out at them that they had been blooming all year, through all seasons. No flower or shrub on Karemoana was prepared to stand alone, to identify spring.

"We've great weather here," the carrier said. "But the water supply's iffy in the summer. Not that it doesn't rain, but the rain seems to drift over the island, to fall in the sea. I wonder how you'll like it here?"

He glanced around the sitting room and Malfred saw his curiosity and puzzlement. "You're a painter? They told me you were a retired schoolteacher."

So "they" had been busy already!

"You want to lock your doors at night. Nobody's wanting to scare you but there's an element of this island, an element . . ." He spoke as if he were quoting some authority, and as if, in quoting, he were trying to disentangle or mingle the two meanings of "element" that were uppermost in his and Malfred's minds.

"Yes, I'd lock your doors all right."

The carrier left by the front door, stopping once again to remark on the fine spring day.

I'm not afraid of any "element" Malfred thought as she watched him go.

What a wonderful view over the gulf! How beautiful the gorse and manuka! But they tell nothing; they've bloomed all year; they're casual, blasé; one gets from contemplating them, not the expected delight in spring blossom but perhaps the feeling of horror roused by the prospect of everlasting life, as if this island were an island of the Gods where the inhabitants stay young, paralyzed in growth, like the lovers on the Grecian Urn, and where the flowers are never buds, never drop their withered petals, but stay for ever in full bloom. Thus my fancy goes.

Then Malfred shut the front door, quickly, and leaned against it, as if trying to keep out something or someone that might enter out of necessity or malice or habit.

An element? What type of element?

"Deceased estate," she said, beginning to arrange her lighter pieces of furniture. "And no relatives to claim her few belongings."

She picked up the pile of small, leatherbound, poetry books lying on the built-in bookcase.

The Eve of St. Agnes. To Nora from father.

They told her how, upon St. Agnes' Eve,
Young virgins might have visions of delight,
And soft adorings from their loves receive
Upon the honeyed middle of the night, . . .

Then—Matthew Arnold.

Is it so small a thing to have enjoyed the sun
To have lived light in the Spring?

Sonnets from the Portuguese.

The face of all the world is changed, I think,
Since first I heard the footsteps of thy soul.

One and sixpenny leatherbound dreams exchanged, Malfred knew, who remembered, as birthday or Christmas presents between the young and trembling. She remembered a sentence from a textbook of Animal Physiology— "In all vertebrates except the degenerate sea squirt each individual arises by the union of male and female." The sea squirt, poor sea squirt, was indeed degenerate, not having known *Sonnets from the Portuguese,* or Madeline's dream on *The Eve of St. Agnes!*

Hastily, with some sense of neighboring rivalry, Malfred stood the few books side by side on the shelf, and began to arrange her own books. They were few, read narrowly, deeply, not often. Sometimes she read for the pleasure of reading; other times a ham sandwich would have served her just as well, for she had acquired, as everyone does, a mixture and replacement of habits, and since the habit of literacy was accepted, it had been included in her routine along with sleeping and eating and other satisfactions. She took care to put on her bedside table one of the big *Beautiful New Zealand* books of colored photographs and vivid text. (These were published regularly, with the latest, most fashionable author writing words to fit the spectacular scenery portrayed in the photographs.) Another book for her bedside was one of *Paintings of the New Zealand Scene,* where there were few people but many mountains, natural lakes, rivers, plains, all depicted faithfully, realistically, after the school that Malfred had followed in her life as a Sunday painter.

Then she chose the paintings she would hang. One of her own—*The Mouth of the Waitaki.* Others of scenes around Matuatangi painted by fellow members of the Matuatangi Art

43

Society. Then there were photos to be arranged: Mother, Father, Graham, Fernie, Oliver, Lucy, Roland, Fernie's sons and daughter. She decided against Wilfred, the lost lover, whose photo she had kept chiefly, though she did not care to admit this, to aid her memory when she felt in a sentimental mood. She realized that when people die, even those one has loved dearly, their image fades in time. It seems an insult to their memory to admit even in private that the loved face is blurred, the voice indistinct. The plea for a "likeness" of the loved one had its ulterior motive!

Moving about from room to room, making her bed, arranging her toilet things, setting furniture here and there, sometimes opening the front door to look again upon the view of the gulf, inspecting the cupboards in the kitchen, then hurrying into the garden to discover the boundaries of her section, the lemon tree, the orange tree, the fig tree, the ice plant sprawled across the back grass, the clothesline, propped by a manuka branch, the remains of the old well, the two tanks—one, concrete, sunk in the earth, half-filled with clear water and lined with leaf-mould and gray mud, the other, rusted, propped on a decaying frame; returning to the house to make sure she had made the correct decisions and arrangements, she became more and more aware of the busyness that served as a useful but depressing lid to emptiness. She knew that in setting her easel near the window of the small bedroom and placing her paints, rags, paper, canvas, she made more movements with her arms and her body than were necessary. She was engaged in a kind of physical verbosity designed to conceal a dread silence and stillness. Her life at that moment seemed like a toy which had come at last to rest but which whirred, rattled, clicked, because it could not recognize or accept the condition of rest.

Suddenly she was still. Her arms drooped by her side. Her head poked forward. Her breasts drooped and swung like the blue ice plants that hung from the grassy bank outside the kitchen window. Her legs were apart. Her back humped. Let no one say that the attitude of rest is always beautiful. Yet now, perhaps for the first time in her fifty-three years, Malfred Signal was alone, in charge, and at rest.

She allowed herself, before sleep that night, the unusual bounty of a memory that came without regret or longing, expressed by someone who, like herself, had been bound hand and foot for the first half of her life, though in her case the bonds had been literal, the escape had been earlier, and the evidence of the escape had become a remembered part of history. Also, in this case, the freedom had been given not by death, though this had been feared even by Miss Barrett (More tea, Miss Cunningham? Do you take sugar and milk, Miss Humphrey?) and those who *surrounded* her.

So weeping, how a mystic Shape did move
Behind me, and drew me backward by the hair;
And a voice said in mastery, while I strove—
"Guess now who holds thee?"—"Death," I said. But there,
The silver answer rang, "Not Death, but Love."

How everlasting was the dream in the human mind that some agent, some time that was never too late, would bring the permanent longed-for release from imprisonment! The dream and the delusion gave interest to all myths and legends. So often faith was put in another human being, neighbor or stranger, as the agent; or in a God; the restlessness to be what one was not remained so often a restlessness, until dreams took over, or until some part of the body or mind, unbound, made assault, creative or destructive, on the limiting environment, appeased by habit or inertia into a comfortable state of being "at home" to human imprisonment.

So Malfred read, before sleeping, remote from her former desires, her age having placed her in many ways, not in all, beyond the sex barrier, the words of that other woman who had been set free. (She understood, now, the close interest that members of the staff had always shown in discussions, books, films, about Elizabeth Barrett. It was a more hopeful dream for them to inhabit than that of the Sleeping Beauty!)

So Malfred's reading began as the pleasant indulgence of one who is at last alone, in charge, and at rest.

> *Go from me. Yet I feel that I shall stand*
> *Henceforward in thy shadow. Nevermore*
> *Alone upon the threshold of my door*
> *Of individual life, I shall command*
> *The uses of my soul, nor lift my hand*
> *Serenely in the sunshine as before,*
> *Without the sense of that which I forbore—*
> *Thy touch upon the palm. The widest land*
> *Doom takes to part us, leaves thy heart in mine*
> *With pulses that beat double. What I do*
> *And what I dream include thee, as the wine*
> *Must taste of its own grapes. And when I sue*
> *God for myself, He hears that name of thine,*
> *And sees within my eyes the tears of two.*

The emphasis upon the word "touch" pleased Malfred. So often it was merely the touch of the agent that released the prisoner into happiness—or new suffering, new prisons. The Golden

Touch. The Fairy Wand. The games played by children, Tiggy-Tiggy-Touch, touch flesh or wood; but touch; the world or the wheel going round and round and the need for "somebody" to "touch."

Could the release given by death, by her mother's death, promise a lifetime bounty? Malfred wondered. Death was a cold touch to be used for release into Life. Had she mistaken the door? Was she stepping backwards into darkness and isolation? Why had she chosen an island in which to live? Did she hope that some creature would emerge to her from the encircling sea? Had she set herself in isolation in deliberate hope that the "touch" of human or divine agent would be more marked, more dramatic? Was she trying to re-enact a legend? And what was the meaning or urgency of the legend when the chief character was a middle-aged, retired, Art teacher from the provincial, prejudiced, puritanical background of Matuatangi where few eyes looked further than their own front lawn and their motor mower, and those who gazed out to sea kept to the three-mile-limit set by law, not by vision, and did not recognize the signs of the new migration, did not observe the waves crowded with fleets of hungry minds for whom literacy was not a casual ham sandwich on the laden (overladen) lunch table, but the first violently snatched and coveted crust of bread?

Such thoughts, unknown to Malfred before, were troubling to one who had imagined herself to be at last free, in charge, and at rest!

·9·

SHE WONDERED WHAT HAD caused the invasion. The old clichés, quoted in newspapers, magazines, Parliament, came to her mind: "The world is getting smaller." "Modern means of travel." There's "increased consciousness" of the "human dilemma." "Nations can no longer bury their heads in the sand." And so on.

There was some truth in these. The world had indeed become afflicted with an epidemic of awareness that was most likely to attack those, like Malfred, who lived alone, for they (and she) had not their vision blocked by the nearness of demanding relatives—how mountainous her mother had been! Certainly others, like Malfred, who lived alone, looked with more love on cats, dogs, birds, and planned to make provision for them, and were entitled to do so; but awareness of the human family, fast-spreading, was incurable; and the fact that it was looked on as a disease was strengthened by the many efforts made to get rid of it. Oh, if only I didn't know! Pandora voiced the same complaint. *I want to know, I know, I want not to know.* The cycle was relentless. *I want to see, I see, I want not to see.* It seemed at times that all living was directed towards completing the final stage of the cycle—*I want not to.* Yet knowledge was always the victor in its invasion, in spite of the many fortresses, defenses, maintaining of so-called strategic positions—if only the Defense Budget of the human mind and heart could be made public, the history written of the battles, the wars, defeats and victories! And how many small minds, and islands, like Karemoana, had struggled for centuries to resist the invaders, whether they were forces of love, hate, knowledge, awareness?

It was love that could be named as the most treacherous invader. The human make-up had decreed it the most wanted. Its disguise was the most complete. It was the fifth column, the underground movement. And how bitter and useless was the struggle to get rid of it and all that it brought with it! In the calendar of love the day before, the day after were strangers. How cunning but mistaken the philosophers were who tried to set the past and the present on the same foundation, who insisted the child was father of the man when it was not so, when the two were related only in that they were both members of the human family. The child was father of the man only, as Lear's daughters suggested of their father, to care for him in his dotage—of age or of love. The moment after love made its invasion the child and the man were strangers, separate. And if love never made its invasion? Then one carried the dead child in one's life, daily waking and sleeping.

Malfred had known love—was there anyone who had not? At fifty-three she could look back on it, if she cared to, and trace the physical outline of the wall it had built between moment and moment. Because it had been so fleeting a human association, because her lover had not stayed, when the mountains, the sea, the bush, the rivers had stayed, and the nor'wester blowing across the plains, and the bitter east wind from the sea, and even the houses had stayed, and the towns with their shops in them, and the models in the shop windows, and the Council Meetings and the clubs, and the school with its classroom, the paintpots, the brushes, the staffroom, the gossip over morning tea—because almost everything had stayed, Malfred had carefully changed the label that hung in the vacant love-place, *Human Being,* to read, *Almost Everything.* And then, how passionately she had felt towards the beautiful bush, the rivers, the trees! And how the images crowded in her mind of the fists of snowgrass, full of snow, thrust into the open mouth of the sky!

That had been the physical invasion of love. The invasion of the mind had been more gradual, less spectacular, not related to any one person. Its chief enemy had been habit, routine, inertia. Yet Malfred knew that her desire, coming so late in life, for "freedom" would not have seemed so dramatic, so urgent, had she not experienced the many years of imaginative sleep. A hibernating animal, she thought, waking in spring, would find in itself a similar store of the kind of energy and strength that would help it to make changes in its life, to migrate to a new home. Whereas such an animal had been kept alive by the supply of food in its body and in the small cache beside it in the hollow tree or burrow, she had been fed by an accumulation of habits, that, contrary to the lore of dieticians, provide most nourishment for the human race. And her waking, Malfred wondered, that she had found when her mother died, was it the release that so many people hoped for at their own death, after a lifetime of sleep? And yet was this lifetime of sleep in itself not imposed by necessity, by the dreadful sickness of being alive that needed to be cured by a form of hibernation?

Malfred remembered the words of one of her favorite poems:

> *Lucky indeed*
> *The rampant suffering suffocating jelly*
> *Burgeoning in pools, lapping the grits of the desert,*
> *The elementary sensual cures,*
> *The hibernations and the growth of hair assuage:*
> *Or best of all the mineral stars disintegrating quietly into light.*

"Lucky" was a well-chosen word, Malfred thought. Her own release or waking from hibernation, indeed her own hibernation, had been, perhaps, just "luck." She smiled to think of the reaction of her family if she had turned to them at her mother's funeral and remarked, "How lucky that mother has died!"

And thus the first night of Malfred's stay in her new home was spent not in the promised blissful sleep, with the sound of the sea and the sea wind in her ears, but in a turmoil of waking and thinking and wondering; with the strange feelings that an animal might have known, an animal no longer young, falling asleep in frost and snow, waking to spring and bright sunlight.

Sometimes, through the hours that had begun to seem so long, she switched on the light above her bed and studied her new bedroom. The softboard walls, painted light blue, had scars that showed the room had once been the kitchen of the bach. A tap with a notice, "Please Do Not Use," projected from one wall. Where the back door had been was a rectangular shape covered with embossed wallpaper. Former light fittings had been removed from the ceiling, rearranged to fit the room's new purpose. Shelves had been built along the narrow window that looked out, down the grassy path, to the white-painted letterbox with its new milk-flag (a strip of old pillowcase) flying. The built-in wardrobe had two holes in the floor, plugged, one with a thick piece of wood, the other with a crumpled rag; beside the holes someone—the former owner?—had left a small tin lid filled with grain: rat poison. A thin, pink cardigan and a shapeless, flowered, summer dress or smock hung in the wardrobe.

Over the four walls of the bedroom there were marks of drawing pins; cellotape that had been stuck on, pulled off, removing the paint with it; and insulated hooks.

Lying in bed, with one of the curtains drawn back across the window, Malfred had the feeling that she could walk out the window straight into the sea; only the sea was visible from where she lay: a dark purple mass, with one or two withered flax stems pressed so close against the window pane that they belonged inside the room rather than outside with the sea. There was a shuffling, raking sound as of gravel being distributed on a garden path; a soft hissing, like wet leaves beginning to burn. Then, towards morning, as the wind began to rise, the house began to shake, the wind screamed in the telephone and electric wires outside and thudded, like a heavy body, against the windows. Again and again. Malfred switched on the light. She looked, wondered, listened. With such wide horizons before her window it seemed that the whole world ranged itself along the horizon's rim, gazing towards Karemoana, with the relentless questioning that characterizes the whole world. Tell. Tell. Answer or else. Give. The beam of light that came suddenly through the window was the moon, hastily bundled in rags of cloud, and thrust into darkness.

Malfred felt tired now. The irritating grain of sleep that comes into the eyes with tiredness made her blink and rub the corners of her eyes. Then suddenly she slept.

·10·

THE NEXT DAY WAS spent in domestic investigation; who sold what and where, where could this and that be found. On her walk into the township of Kare at about noon Malfred encountered most of the people who lived permanently on the island: middle-aged, elderly gray-haired women wearing brogues with ribbed soles, tweed skirts, headscarves; retired teachers of Music, Art, Language; retired women doctors; clerks; elderly men whose past calling was less evident; gray-haired men with sticks to help them walk; couples with lined, tired faces; then, apart still, studying, criticizing, learning to love and hate their new home, the immigrants—English, Irish, Scottish, Dutch, Polish. There seemed to be few Maoris on the island that had once been the home of the first moa-hunters. People smiled at Malfred and she returned their smiles. They spoke of the weather. It was an early spring, they said. Their daffodils had long withered. But the storms were to come: rain, hail, sleet, gales. Karemoana was a beautiful place —did she not think? Indeed it was beautiful, they said, but they had lived on the island sixteen, twenty years, and were tired of it; but of course it was beautiful. Only there was no downtown; there was nothing, in the end, but wind and sea; even the island itself was a mere convenience for the wind and the sea. Now on the mainland. . . .

So they were selling out, they said. They were leaving. The place was rural, backward, the shops were poorly stocked; but above all, every window they looked out of, they saw the sea.

"I don't think," Malfred said, "that I would get tired of look-ing at the sea."

They spoke as if they humored her.

"You might not," they said. "You might not. But when you have lived here ten to twenty years, *then* you'll be able to judge."

In a way, Malfred had already made a judgment which she did not communicate to people she met. It was: the islanders are old, tired, preyed upon by the sea. Where is the vision of perpetual youth, where are the lovers, the frozen blooms on the Grecian Urn?

Most of the islanders have built their homes to get a "view" of the sea, and now they are haunted by it. Living on an island, one can escape only by diving into the sea; it is like being a swimmer surrounded by sharks, keeping the sharks at bay, yet knowing that one false move, one lapse, and the sharks—and here the sea—will close in for the kill. Perhaps even now, as the sharks

smell blood, the sea could sense the way these islanders had cast
away their former illusions.

Malfred walked in the one street of Kare where there were
shops, a Post Office, a Bank, a picture theater with a Greek name
and the appearance of an outsize public lavatory, squatting on
the corner. Few of the houses lining the streets were occupied;
they were summer baches, windows shut, blinds drawn; many of
the people walking in the street had grown to look like the
summer baches: there was an appearance of rust in their skin and
eyes; an unoccupied look on their faces. Perhaps, Malfred wondered, this was immortality? The vision was this street, not the
scene on the Grecian Urn. And one could grow tired of immortality, one could plead to die because one was not doomed to do
so.

She went to the Post Office and bought stamps. She had no
letters to write or post, she expected to receive few letters, once
her absence in Matuatangi had become accepted; yet it seemed
important that she should be on friendly terms with the postal
clerks who were both middle-aged, gaunt, formidable women.
She inquired— Was there a police station? How was the law
enforced on the island? And the doctor—who, where was he,
what were his hours? The District Nurse? Was there a district
nurse?

Finally, as part of her act of settling in, she rang the Auckland
Telephone Exchange. She had just moved into her home on
Karemoana, she told the operator, she had a telephone but no
number, could they give her a number? She was a retired woman,
living by herself. She had been told there was an "element" on
the island. She needed the telephone in case of emergency. Did
they not agree with her? They were sorry, the operator said, there

was a long waiting list. Besides, the island was being connected in a few months' time to the Mainland Exchange and it would not be practicable to begin granting numbers that would so soon have to be changed.

For someone, Malfred told herself, who has retired, to contemplate the natural scene, I'm going to extraordinary lengths to make sure I'm in touch with people. Post Office. Police. Doctor. Telephone.

She did not explore the matter. I'm just being a good citizen, she told herself complacently, but she felt a wave of depression and tiredness as she came out of the telephone box and saw the few people, with so much air between them, more air than people, dominant air, sea, sky; what hope was there of living anywhere in this country unless one submitted, as Malfred had done, to the invasion and the terms of the treaty that followed: there were to be no people. Sea, sky, bush, mountains, rivers; and no people.

·11·

ON THE AFTERNOON of the fifth day Malfred felt at the tips of her fingers the urge that came when she needed to paint. This desire to touch paint, paper, canvas, if necessary to finger-paint, through a modesty that she had recognized, sadly, long ago as incompatible with real talent, made her prefer to paint, as it were, by proxy, using a brush or pencil. As for cycling over her work or stamping in rage upon it, both were out of the question. She realized, though, that the personal involvement of parts of the body with painting (fingers were not the only or chief human protuberances) tended to give the artist a Little-Jack-Horner self-satisfaction that was scarcely related to the finished work: the artist, like Little Jack Horner when he removed the plum from the pie, was taking something from his work rather than giving to it.

In her anxiety to begin Malfred pinned a sheet of drawing paper on the easel and squeezed the paint from a box of tempera colors that might have been used by a child, for she had found them in the bach, on the mantelpiece: doll-sized tubes—Chinese White, Lemon Yellow, Chrome Yellow, Vermilion, Carmine, Burnt Sienna, Chrome Green, Cobalt Blue, Prussian Blue . . . the names were enough to set her dreaming again. Her first impulse that came easily along its well-worn track was to look out of the window, to look from sea to paper to sea, to paint the sea, blinking her eye, like the shutter of a camera, capturing its agreed appearance, shape, form, texture. How satisfied she had felt at the Art Society's Exhibition when a visitor, seeing her work, exclaimed, "But it's *exactly* like the— (river or mountain or picnic scene). I'd recognize the spot *anywhere!*"

Then another impulse, traveling more slowly but persistently, came to her. She took two tubes of lanolin—relics of her past life that only a strong sense of economy, the desire to hoard, characteristic of approaching age, had persuaded her to bring with her; and mixing the available blues, greens, whites, she painted the sea at that moment as she felt and saw it.

The sickly smell of the lanolin made her shut her eyes with remembered horror. There was no foam on the real sea like that which frothed its creamy sweetness, smelling of death, on those blue and green waves flowing in from the wide oceans of the world. The lanolin blossomed as death had blossomed in the last hour of old Mrs. Signal's dying. When Malfred finished the painting she tried to tell herself that the lanolin had been a substance in the paper, had oozed out of it as she began to paint.

She was no more brave or cowardly than other people. She wanted to take away from herself the responsibility for what she had done. She knew, at this moment, though in her life at Matuatangi she had not known it, that an artist dreads most of all not publicity nor criticism nor oblivion but the burden of the responsibility of having painted what he has painted. His work can rise more accusingly than any child who cries, "You conceived me!" to say, "You painted me; you wrote, composed me!" An artist must live always with this accusation. A painting doesn't leave the household, get married, get drunk, drown its sorrows; a painting doesn't grow up; it stays, it stays.

Explaining her afternoon to herself Malfred said, "I went into the bathroom, and from the shelf where I noticed there are spider webs, spiders, slaters, too many for my liking, I took tubes of lanolin which I mixed with tempera paint. Then I painted the sea. I have called my painting 'My Last Days in Matuatangi.' There are no people in my painting. No one could make out in this foam of lanolin the arm of someone being drawn under by the waves. Not even the bereaved mockingbird in search of its love could find it fluttering in this storm of lanolin. There are no people in my painting. *No people.*"

The storm came that night. Without warning. Malfred lay in bed. Outside there was the rhythmic hush of the sea, the crackle of flax leaves, the jab-jab pecking against the wall of the black-beaked flax flowers. She could feel the faint shudder as the wind, still gentle, turned the corner from the front to the side of the bach. It was a surrounding wind, trailing bonds that encircled the bach. It was a warm, mild wind. It brought the smell of daffodils and wattle and gorse, and the promise of an early summer with the more spectacular subtropical flowers, bright red and yellow; big flowers, striped, brilliant, like sun umbrellas; giant fuchsia, frangipani, jacaranda; blooms that Malfred knew from the gardens of fiction or the more limited hothouses in the Botanical Gardens. How did one feel, she wondered, looking from one's window onto the flame of a frangipani? Such a life seemed dreamlike; Malfred feared the strangeness of it; in an inexplicable way she felt that her life was "too late" for "that kind of flower." Oh, "up north" was everything that those who lived "down south" had described to her! For a moment she had had a small taste only of the subtropical world. Soon, besides the flowers, she would know the insects—mosquitoes, cicadas, crickets, ants. Already, out of the new world, there was one plant that haunted her, that she knew she must paint: the mangrove in its sordid, calm, sinister bed of gray mud; its harsh dusty leaves; the straightness of its stem; the scene, twice a day when the tide came in, of the almost submerged plants, like sinister evidence of a drowned miniature forest. Karemoana, on the part of the island that faced the mainland had just such a desolate mangrove swamp. Malfred had found it in a short walk the evening before, when the high road, in view of the sea, descended slowly towards the mainland side of the island where, suddenly, the holiday baches had a derelict appearance that seemed not to be the result of their winter desertion but of their nearness to the mangrove swamp. Some of the baches were occupied. Malfred saw two families of children, Maori and Pakeha, playing near the swamp. She was surprised at their ragged patched clothes, their thin faces and limbs; she had forgotten about poverty and, until now, no one had reminded her. She felt as she heard and watched their gun-battle—the dead lying so still, so close to the swamp—that of all the plants "up north" and "down south" it was the mangroves

that had the power to lure poverty, as a kind of human complement to their own vegetable squalor. On Karemoana it would be
at this meeting-place of sea and swamp, this expanse of dust-gray
estuary near mangrove forests, that the ragged would always
play; and they would be outcasts as the mangroves were outcasts
in such a bounteous land of light and color. Or did the mangroves, like the twisted tough pohutukawas, flower at some other
time during the year? No one could tell, looking at the winter
pohutukawa, the coast tree, wind-fighting, gnarled, sprawling
without decoration, that in summer it would burst into flame
and its flowers would die in a carpet of crimson ashes. Nor,
perhaps, did anyone know the ultimate bloom of poverty, nor in
what season of year or life it would flourish.

A gust of wind sprang, thudded like an animal against the
window. Malfred felt her heart beating fast with apprehension.
The storm had worsened; the wind had divided itself now into
upper and lower layers, the lower consisting of a hurling weight,
attacking the lower windows and foundations of the house, a
being whose harsh breath could be felt and heard; an upper
layer, more agile, treading its prowling earthbound brother with
equestrian lightness, whirling, dancing, then with an abandon-
ment of screaming, hurling itself, too, against the windows and
walls of the house. It seemed to Malfred as if the whole world lay
without, trying to get in. Looking around the room, at the
anemone-patterned curtains, the basket chair, the table, the bed,
the torn ceiling from which a former light fitting had been
wrenched to make way for "alterations," Malfred was overcome
by the sense of the insubstantiality of the visible and tangible.
The essence of the room hollowed itself out to leave a gap like a

wound, like the dark hole in the ceiling. The whole world lay without; within, there was nothing. Malfred felt she could have reached over to the basket chair and thrust her fist through it; the weave would have melted or vanished at her touch; the table flowed, the curtains hid nothing, were nothing. The enormity of what lay outside began to touch Malfred with a cold brand that slid in a snail-track of sweat across her forehead. She listened intently. I must distinguish the sound of the sea, she thought. I must make something rational, eternal, from this animal scream-ing. In all the storms I have known down south, wind, rain, snow, I never knew this island terror. The violent, snow-fed Waitaki that I respect and love for its power never made war on me and my home in this way. The natural scene that I love, that I've painted faithfully all my life, never turned against me like this. Have I not the right to be shocked and fearful? Unlike Lear, I *have given* the wind, the sea, the sky, the trees my kingdom; I have called them, not children, perhaps lovers; perhaps, there-fore, they have a right to turn against me. Yet I'm afraid there may be a point reached in chaos, a climax of chaos that will emit life, like fumes of the storm; a human beginning thrust from the inhuman natural scene.

At least I have electric light in my house. Returning to con-template home comforts, she switched the bedlamp off and on and off to reassure herself. "There may be lightning," she thought. "I must prepare for sudden darkness." She spoke aloud, and almost as soon as she spoke she heard a sound, a swishing, as of footsteps on grass, and a thunderous determined knocking on the back door. She held her breath, then sighed a long, slow sigh. Twenty-five years ago, she thought, excitement would have pierced her at that moment like pieces of sharp yellow glass with all the jagged possible perils of youth. Now, in spite of her apprehension, her fast-beating heart, she felt no sharpness of feeling. The excitement lay knotted within her, like tired long-used veins. Its flow was halting. Age had put up so many barriers; the underground rivers were trickling channels. Her excitement had, as it were, no plans about its destination; there was no sudden blush on her cheeks—only a diffused dampness on the palms of her hands and the soles of her feet and the body smell that used to be daisies, ordinary spring daisies, but was now the nasty stench of dog daisies. The knocking sounded again. Who could it be? Of course I won't answer, she thought. It could be anyone. It's dark and it could be anyone. Who could it be, at this hour?

She looked at her watch. Ten past ten.

Perhaps I imagined the knocking. There's so much noise. And the storm, the wind, the sea. No one would want to visit me at this hour on such a night. That is, no one but—no one but—

She switched off her light and prepared to sleep, and then, in a lull in the wind's screaming, she heard again the swishing as of footsteps in the grass outside her window, and again the knocking, determined, louder, beating on the back door. Had she taken the key from the door? she wondered. It was said that if a key were left in a locked door intruders could manipulate the key in such a way as to gain an entry. Breathlessly, she crept from her bed, silently opened the kitchen door, seized the length of string dangling from the key and withdrew the key from the back door. She crept back to the bed and lay with her head leaning against the wall. She was panting. She knew then that she was afraid. It was not the wild fear that she might have known years ago in the same situation: that kind of fear was exciting, defiant, demanding action. This fear was resigned, it existed in the room with her as an accepted companion; had she been a poet she might have addressed it in the same intimate terms that the poet addressed his fancy: "Hello, my fear, whither goest thou?" It was still the old fear of the unknown. Malfred had learned that as she grew older and knew more, by choice or force or chance, the area of the unknown did not therefore diminish, as there was no way of separating finite from infinite knowledge. Even the most trivial fact, when examined, was found to carry an unidentifiable growth of darkness not recorded in any physiognomy of knowing. One feared other people, beasts, Gods, isolated powers; and oneself. One feared, one hoped too: who knocked? Who or what wanted so desperately to get in that a night of storm had been defied or ignored?

Listening, she had not time to let her fear make way for fantasy, though she remembered the knocking on the gate in *Macbeth:* "Whence is that knocking that so appalls?" and she thought of the wartime game that her pupils had played during air-raid practice: Knock Knock. Who's there? A game where the fear was hidden in lightheartedness. They'd had one air-raid practice, that time when submarines had been lurking in Auckland Harbor, and the whole school had gone to the dugouts in the side of the hill behind Matuatangi, and Malfred, in charge of the fourth form, had suggested party games; and had threatened— yes, threatened, for art lessons were chiefly a threat in those days —that when the girls returned to the classroom they would be asked to "paint or draw the scene in the air-raid shelter." Some of the girls had been embarrassed at having to hide from a possible enemy, at having to pretend—for their days of public pretense were past—that they were in mortal danger. They had sung songs, war songs, the kind that in the future they would recall with horror, if their consciences and human sympathies had developed.

There's a war in Abyssinia, won't you come,
There's a war in Abyssinia won't you come,
Mussolini will be there
Shooting peanuts in the air,
There's a war in Abyssinia won't you come.

and

Run rabbit run rabbit run run run
We'll give old Hitler his fun fun fun,
He'll get by without his rabbit pie
So run rabbit run rabbit run . . .

These and other songs making a game of war; the kind of song that in wartime served the same purpose as the scream accompanying the bayonet attack.

At the beginning of the war, after the first echelon had sailed away in a glory of *Now Is the Hour* and *Maori Battalion March to Victory,* and the first casualty lists appeared in the newspapers, Malfred became one of the many schoolteachers, unmarried, who throughout their career attract the rumor, fantasy or fact, that their "boys" died in the war. A class of fourth-formers with thoughts of their first dance at the Boys' High and promise of petting parties out the "Willows," had to find some explanation for a schoolteacher with no husband or children; and the explanation had to be particularly convincing if, like Malfred Signal, the teacher in question could not have been described as ugly. In schoolgirl fantasy, as in folklore, the ugly deserve and get few rewards.

Wilfred had been killed in the war in North Africa. Malfred thought of him now as part of the desert, and she wondered, in her less sentimental moods, if his return to New Zealand to take over his father's farm in the country back of Matuatangi and his life between Five Hills and Matuatangi, between sheep and Malfred (their engagement had been unofficial; they had left each other, in the delusive way such states are described, as "free") would have had a similar effect of distributing his remains in a different but no less final desert.

Malfred remembered her feelings in the air-raid shelter (she had heard the news about Wilfred that day) and the scene of the girls singing and playing *Knock Knock who's there? Knock knock who's there?* Whoever invented a door invented also the fear or hope that someone or something would plead for the door to be opened. The game the girls played was a party game, but perhaps it was also a game of fear, of wondering. When they returned to the classroom and the threat of having them "paint or draw the scene" was carried out, their work had shown no promise or originality. They had never known an air-raid warning; how could they be expected to portray, vividly, "Scene in an Air-Raid Shelter"? The paintings were cheerful—in bright primary colors; the scenes were almost without exception party scenes; the faces were laughing faces. It was no use trying to make the girls *feel* a horror they had not experienced, to inject them with horror as a hunter now gives an injection of stimulant or tranquilizer to the beasts in his charge. (Malfred wondered, at times, if the schoolgirls were other than animals. She had less definite thoughts on herself, the Art mistress, in the role of huntress.) Malfred remembered that during the war she and other members of the staff had pottered about the staffroom excusing everyone who showed lack of feeling or understanding by the plea, "They just don't realize." This excusing was done for children and adults alike: "They don't realize; it's not their fault."

She knew now that she herself had never *realized*—where realization is a form of turning understanding, vague sympathies, into compulsory currency, to be given away in the streets to anyone who passes, that is, to the *neighbor*. She had studied Henry Moore's *Sketches* made in air-raid shelters, had seen the tired suffering faces, had known that the poverty of hope and comfort had been emphasized by the abundance of gentle curves drawn by the artist, by the pastel shades, not used, as in the work of the schoolgirls, as colors that were what they seemed to be, but used in a way that drew attention not to the pinks and blues themselves, the cosy, infant first-colors, but to the dark, deprived, old-man, old-woman areas lying behind the nursery gentleness. It was as if the artist were saying, "Yes, Yes," with such skill that his message was heard as a depressing cry of anguish, "No, no! No, no!" The colors beyond these comfortable pinks and blues were not opposites or complements; they were desolate, unknown colors: the dark sides of moons where, in full shining view of the world, there was such sport that little dogs laughed!

Malfred had enough imagination to grasp part of the message of the drawings. She felt depressed when she needed so often to excuse the girls and the staff and members of the community because they did not "realize." With the girls, the excuses came easily: their minds and hearts were not fully developed. It was harder to think the same of mayors and councilors and neighbors, or if one did think the same and made it known, it was not only hard, but libelous and costly. Malfred knew, when she made up her mind to set out for her island home, that she had wasted most of her life making excuses for herself and for others, by saying that her and their endowment of realization had been slight, that in an isolated, prosperous, well-fed country that had known one depression but had not known war among its civilian population, what could one expect but a lack of realization, a shallowness of feeling? After all, one had to suffer to . . .

So, year after year, the old clichés had fallen from Malfred's lips onto others, and from others' lips onto her. She read the words in the newspaper, heard them over the wireless (before its name was changed to radio), heard them in the House of Representatives. And even now, if one of the excuses, that of "isolation" was being discarded, that had the effect only of increasing the weight and repetition of the others. We're a prosperous well-fed country. . . . It's hard for us to realize . . . after all, one must suffer to . . .

Knowing that one has wasted almost a lifetime living in restricted awareness can be a source of agony while it promises both future ecstasy and agony. The usual longing is to forget what one knows, to be made less aware. The classic example is of the woman who falling asleep one night, longing to forget "self and all," woke the next morning to have no knowledge or memory. Memory is a subversive force, allied to strong feeling. In a way less spectacular the same little war goes on from day to day.

Malfred had fallen asleep with a longing to know, to be aware, and had woken in the fullest state of awareness, of remembering, of knowing.

The grindstones that sharpen the senses—conversion, sexual or filial love, extremes of human relations, environment, heredity—

are not given to everyone. This, again, until Malfred's decision to live on Karemoana had been, for her, a ready excuse for not "realizing" so many things. She feared now, that having torn apart the excuses, she would not be able to confront the ordinary "day to day" living that takes no account of self-styled visionaries, of women in middle age who decide to "see" when their seeing has changed to include a world they never dreamed of before. She felt guilty, too, that her wasted years had not been spent in teaching her pupils to "see." She was overawed by the imaginative force that must be rallied so that her country would be peopled by human beings and neighbors. Where was the Ministry of Imagination? The Secretary of Empathy? Because her country had had so little direct experience of the hunger and fear that were the daily life of millions of people in the world, it had to increase, train, its imaginative force; even in its lack it had the power to produce an overwhelming force of imaginative experts, trained to see the invisible, the intangible, the real.

If I write to Parliament in this way, Malfred thought, they'll say I'm a crank. Perhaps I am. Perhaps I'm too old to try to change the way of seeing. Yet I have this dream of a vast imaginative force, its wealth drawn from its initial poverty, that quells prejudice, suspicion, that acts as a beam to draw distant countries close, so that each sees, with instinctive vision, the needs of the other. Perhaps they may say I'm only another middle-aged spinster "gone missionary"; but the missioning part does not concern me; it's the seeing. It's appalling that I've spent a lifetime with the direct opportunity of teaching children to see, and that I've wasted almost every hour; more than wasted—I've trained my pupils to see in the same unimaginative way. "The eye has laws. Keep them," I said. But I forgot that the heart has

laws, sometimes conflicting, to be kept. And the mind has laws.
And I never worked out a system in which all laws could be
respected. I clung to the obvious, the visible, the tangible, the
immediately perceived. I forgot the rebel in the eye, the illusions
that can point the way to truth. My life at Matuatangi could be
portrayed as a series of carefully-shaded fire shovels, coal scuttles,
milk jugs, billies, cups. I might even say that "I have measured
out my life in coffee spoons," though perhaps I should substitute
"fire shovels" for coffee spoons.

And now here I am, alone, by choice, at Karemoana. There's a
storm, it's night, and the knocking keeps on and on.

After a final tremendous pounding on the back door there was
silence. Malfred hoped that whoever had knocked, had gone
away, but her hopes fell when there was again a swish of grass as
of footsteps outside, a pause, and the knocking sounded again,
this time on the front door.

"Perhaps they will break the glass panel?" she thought. She
dared not go into the sitting room for, though the front door
panel was of frosted glass, the intruder (she had made up her
mind that whoever knocked was an unwelcome intruder, a
stranger in the neighborhood) might see her. She could not quite
decide why being seen held such peril unless it was that others
might dose her with her own medicine, might "see" her with a
clarity to which she did not care to expose herself. One could
never tell; surely in one's own home one should be granted the
privacy of not being "seen" by the curious world! It was enough
that one had learned in childhood, and could not quite escape
from the idea, that a God who lived in heaven had a special

privilege of lifting the roofs of houses to see what lay beneath them.

The knocking continued. Every few minutes Malfred held her breath to hear if some other sound accompanied the knocking; a voice or voices. Then once again there came the sound of footsteps in the grass, and the knocking sounded on the back door, in such a demanding rhythm that it seemed to take rightness as its prerogative, condemning Malfred for not answering to its command. "It's a criminal act to refuse to acknowledge my knocking. I demand that the door be opened. I've braved the storm to knock at your door. Why don't you make a sign? Why are you so quiet? Answer, answer!"

I don't answer now, Malfred thought, because I'm afraid. I have built the agent of the knocking into such a powerful figure that I'm afraid. I'm no young girl with conflicting fear and hope of ravishment, in a wild panic that if the stranger gets in something may be "done" to me; though, taking account of my age and modesty, I do hold an image of physical force—the wielding of axes, hammers. It is the first fear, when one person is inside, contained, and others clamor to get in. It may be only someone who has lost his way in the storm, who sees in my home an image of comfort, a fire burning, food cooking. . . . It may be a salesman. There are thousands of reasons for knocking at doors. Must I (an intelligent woman, I hope) torture myself because the knocking happens to be late at night in a storm? Why don't I go now, at once, and open the door? No, no, that would not be wise. Anyone—anyone at all—could be knocking out there.

The category of "anyone" was so vast that Malfred closed her eyes in renewed horror as one by one the dismal citizens of "anyone" trooped past: the greedy, the bestial—all the obviously sinful in human form.

"Yes," Malfred said to herself, giving a small, frightened laugh. "It could be anyone. *Anyone from Anywhere.*"

And because *Anywhere,* also, was such a vast land, Malfred closed her eyes again. If she had thought of *Anywhere* before she left Matuatangi, her image of Matuatangi would have been dominant, with the rest of the world a vague colorful image no further developed than the vision of Samarkand as "golden" or the road to the Isles as "heather-tracked." Now, however, her image of *Anywhere* included the World and beyond it; all countries of all spaces; all stars and planets. She remembered rapping a little girl over the knuckles because the outline of the sketched autumn sycamore leaf and seed had been broken. She remembered, now, the fear she had known at the sight of the leaf and seed not completely imprisoned in a firmly defined BB boundary. The girl had been a fool, of course, playing up. Malfred's control had never been what the headmistress or the inspectors desired. The girl had explained, with much giggling from herself and the others in the class, that the gap was left because a grub had built its nest in the leaf and at some time it might want to escape. Malfred could not answer that except with the "all purpose" answer, dear to schoolteachers of Malfred's generation and to novelists of the *Pshaw, Ugh* group: "*Hmph, Hmph.*"

Looking back, she understood what the girl had meant, though she couldn't quite bring herself to be sorry that she had rapped her over the knuckles. She deserved it! Her lips set primly as she remembered. She wondered where the girl was now. "Norma Barron, why, it was Norma Barron!" She said the name aloud;

there was a slight flush on her cheeks. Perhaps the girl was *Any-where* now!

Anyone from *Anywhere.* From another planet? Was there someone from another planet knocking at her door? That was not impossible, not since the mind was realized to be a Christmas stocking of that stretch material, Imagination, that found itself laden with gifts—the same gifts it had always known, but in-creased in size, accommodated by the stretch material that had one limitation only—it was bound to fit, to follow the size of what lay within it; if it were accepted for a lifetime as a finite material, then nothing could be done. There had to be, from within the parcel, the collection of parcels, a sudden pressure, by calculation or chance, that showed the marvels and potentialities of the enclosing material. So. A creature from outer space knock-ing at the door? The little green man? Green, Malfred supposed, because man had to have some assurance that life and growth were possible beyond his own overcrowded, unbearable planet. He could no longer dream of driving out into the country for weekend peace; he had to make plans for leaving the planet.

Malfred's eyes were closed. She was murmuring, "Anyone from Anywhere, Anyone from Anywhere." She looked at the World, such a neat hollow schoolroom world, with colored squares and writing on it; a touch of the finger could turn it; there was even a device behind it where pencils could be sharpened! What a use-ful World! Then the schoolroom image faded and she saw the ugly, terrifying, beautiful Anywhere, no longer spinning at a touch, but motionless, not round but flat, yet with no danger to the inhabitants of falling over the edge, or of being trapped Down Under; and with no sharpening device.

She was brought back from Anywhere to the image of Anyone

74

when another burst of knocking sounded at the door. She whispered to herself suddenly, "*Anyone* is faceless."

Then she turned, pressing her closed eyes to her pillow, seeing beyond the natural rainbow force that intruded in the image, the faceless *Anyone* who knocked so demandingly at her door. She was truly afraid now, almost with a young girl's fear. The police, she thought. How can I get in touch with the police? There's one policeman on the island. How can I get a message to him?

The faceless *Anyone* persisted, and Malfred felt her head beginning to ache with an old woman's ache that reached out and gripped the roots of her gray hair. She dozed. The wind still screamed. The knocking went on and on.

·12·

SHE MUST HAVE DOZED for five or ten minutes, yet it seemed longer, for there was time, as there is always time, for dreams. She floated on the surface of sleep, her mind congealed and cold like thin slabs of broken ice upon a dark pool. It was on these slabs of ice that the day's feelings and experiences would escape from the vast areas of time surrounding sleep; and escaping there they would drift at their own pace downstream. So she dreamed, forgot her dreams, and woke conscious only of having drifted on a dark surface; and having no inclination to think of rivers of sleep, and of her day's experiences leaping from dream to dream, as Liza leapt from floe to floe, she came nearer home, she saw herself in ordinary domesticity, far, far from history, as an area of fat set and broken in a dark dish of cooled soup. She was tired of the mention of fat. Though she had little, and no surplus, she was tired of the word in newspaper articles, the warnings about it given to the middle-aged, the diagrams of it clinging to her (Yes, the article said, "This means You.") arteries. It was rather to be congratulated, she thought, to have gained entry and set up house in such an exclusive temple as an artery. Sometimes it seemed that perhaps *Arteries* were the New Gods.

She'd had few of the bogies of middle age to contend with, though possibly because her attention had not been directed intimately to another's body and the bodies of children, she had observed her own, perhaps too closely, when it finally decided to give up hope of breeding. All that work! Month after month getting ready for the great moment! It was mad, of course, this hope the body seemed to have until it died; it would not listen to reason. Yet, in a way, its reasoning was deeper, held fast to deeper laws than the reason of the mind. Malfred's body, even in its fifty-third year, had still not given up hope. Even yet, in an odd month, like a churchgoer with news of the Second Coming, it would start up its mechanism to prepare the Way. The Way. I am the Way, the Truth, the Light. Two ministers had called in one week to try to persuade Malfred to join their church. They had remarked, "It is the middle-aged who need God to give them a *purpose*. Now is the time to think of Death and what lies beyond."

No, no, Malfred whispered, jerking her eyes open; listening, listening. Yes, the knocking. After an interval, she heard it again, heavy, repeated, a knocking made by fists rather than knuckles; fists beating and beating on the door. That was the knocking. She was relieved to find that she had dozed for so short a time that the knocking had not ceased into an even more frightening silence. She could have wept, though, for the everlasting nature of it. Why did it not go away?

Then suddenly she realized a change. The wind had died. Except for the faint sound of the sea and the repeated knocking, and the light rustle of flax leaves, outside was calm and quiet. Yes, the wind had died, or gone away, or gone to sleep; perhaps it was only resting. She began to breathe more deeply and peacefully. The knocking had been associated in her mind with the wind. Perhaps it too would go away now. She realized that she had half-believed it to be another manifestation of the storm: sea-roar, wind screaming and wailing; telegraph and electric wires moaning; and knocking, by fists of the storm, upon the cottage door.

But it did not go away. It stayed, and with the surrounding quiet it sounded louder, more impatient. Whoever it is will break the door down soon, Malfred thought. It can't go on and on like this. But it did go on and on. It stayed. First at the back door, then the front, then the back again, with always, in between, the gentle swish as the footsteps moved through the grass. And now Malfred felt more truly alone. The storm surrounding the house had been, as it were, a flattering interest of the outside world, a violent interest, in the little white house on the hill and its new inhabitant. The doors, the walls, the windows, all playing their part, had resisted the wind's pressure; and the roof had kept out the rain; and with each flash of lightning the lights of the bedroom had stayed steadily undimmed; while inside the house, Malfred, playing her part, allied with her new home, had resisted too, had not been lured by the deceits of the storm, not even by the knocking at the door, the storm's nearest approach to human

78

shape. But now the walls, the roof, the windows were silent, unresisting, with nothing to resist. Only Malfred's skin, taut against her flesh, took over the role played by wood, glass, iron, as defensive inviolable membrane. The wind struck no further blows; but the knocking of the fists began to bruise her skin and she began to feel some confusion about whether the visitor demanded entry or exit; whether, indeed, it were visitor or guest.

Then, in the calm, against the rose-patterned print curtains that acted as a screen with the street light glowing upon it, she saw the shadow of a human figure. She could not tell whether it was a man, woman, or child for it was thrown, distorted, upon the curtains where it wavered, fluid, changing shape, the arms growing in size, diminishing, the head ballooning, now like a huge globe, now like the eye of a daisy; the shapeless trunk grew breasts, pointed like the spears of the flax leaves, then obscured, destroyed them. It seemed strange that the shadow and its changing form were thrown upon the curtain by a street light that had its own unrelated position and purpose. The shadows thrown by it were as unheeded as droppings of the Gods. The barrier of things in their isolated worlds that yet protruded unknowingly, for it was supposed they had no knowledge, into other worlds, had never seemed, to Malfred, more vivid and frightening. She remembered Plato's shadows on the cave wall. She wondered what procession of Gods marched, like street lights, through Time, leaving their irrelevant and unregarded shadows—groups of human beings, suffering movements and distortions they could not control—influenced by the procession of marching lights. Until now, Malfred had never really understood the fear of the marching pylons, the landscape crisscrossed with Gods. Electric light poles and lights and wires had been among her first country memories down south; light poles and cabbage trees; both high in the sky, to be gazed up at; the tingling gray-splintered pole; the swishing cabbage leaves like brooms in the sky.

The shadow moved and vanished. Malfred lay as if paralyzed; she could get no message of urgency to her limbs. She wanted to run from the house, to cry out, to scream; she wanted to fetch help. She lay without moving, her heart thudding against her breast, hitting and hurting, as if it were a shape of cast iron. Pain came in with her suddenly-drawn breath, and stayed, moving down her left arm, extending itself like an iron rod. She could feel the pressure of it.

"Oh who can be knocking?" she whispered. "Who is it? Will it go on and on and never stop?"

She wondered if she ought to switch on her bedroom light. The only light burning in the house was the small fifteen watt bulb hung in the alcove of the sitting room. Should she switch it off? Should she, perhaps, shine her torch upon the curtain, or, drawing aside the curtain, shine the light outside, taking care to keep herself beyond its glare?

Unable to bear any longer the calm and the knocking, she turned the knob of her bedside radio and heard in her ear a seductive voice describing, "Your thirty cubic foot Fooderama Automatic Defrost magnetic door control deep freeze unit your thirty foot Fooderama." She switched off the radio. Whoever is knocking will know now that there is someone at home, she thought. They'll know that I'm here, that I've heard their knocking, that I've refused to come to the door; now they'll go away at last, they'll leave me in peace. They? Could there be more than one?

She switched on the radio again. A late-night quiz. In what city and country will the next Olympic games be held? Who are the present holders of the Ranfurly Shield? Where is their next challenge match to be played and against whom? Which horse was sold recently to an owner in the United States, what were the stakes of the race and how much did the horse win for his new owner?

The questions seemed so strange, so unrelated to Karemoana, to the knocking on the door. Malfred turned the knob of the radio. Point of Order. Sugar has gone up, tea has gone up, everything has gone up. And Mr. Speaker does the Honorable Member for Karori know that there are farmers in the Waikato who five years ago held five hundred acres of arable land but who today are lucky to be able to use one hundred acres? Has the Honorable Member seen the acres of land lying under water and silt in the Waikato?

What about the man on a pension? A fixed income? The government Superannuitant?

But we need the Bomb, it's the most powerful deterrent we have. And what about Housing, I say what about housing?

The voices from the House of Representatives were cut off suddenly, the light in the radio and in the alcove of the sitting room went out, and the place was in darkness. The intruder, the visitor, whoever had been knocking at the door, had crept to the front porch, opened the electric meter box, and with a flick of the main switch had plunged the house into darkness while outside, the street light in a state of unknowing that made Malfred want to batter it to death had there been life in it, shone serenely undimmed, commanding, distributing all shadows. Malfred looked into the darkness of her room, at the more clearly illuminated curtains. Had I been blind, she thought, longingly, I would never have known of this. It's so dark. I never knew that night combined with aloneness could be so dark; an extra, fearful dark that the blind, too, must know.

She began to cry. She had not cried for months and her tears did not flow easily. The grains of salt were like sand, rubbing, where her palms were pressed over her face.

part two

•

DARKNESS

·13·

SHE HEARD THE FLAX moving, crackling, as if someone had torn off the spears and was breaking them underfoot. She heard a sound like human breathing, a whispering that was not the sea or the fir trees or the grass; for the wind had vanished so completely that it was hard to believe the stillness. After what had seemed hours of persistent fury, the gale had simply suddenly lost heart and hope, had given up and gone home, wherever home might have been. Malfred felt as if the gale had deserted her. She hoped the intruder would follow its example and go home. Or perhaps it had no home. It. He. She. It must be someone who lives on the island, she thought. One of those louts who break the windows of empty houses, tear down the fences, smash the letter-boxes, drain the water out of tanks, break milk bottles on the roof. The louts. Youths. Delinquents with their strange clothes and stranger language and their cold stare—I've seen the way they look at me and members of my generation, as if it were *our fault, my fault*. As if *what* were my fault? I don't know. The state of things, I suppose. The swamp. The darkness. As if it were we who turned off the light.

Malfred knew there were women of her age who made fools of themselves with the younger generation; who lifted up their skirts and capered about crying, "We understand it all." Also, there were those who made equal fools of themselves by not lifting up their skirts and claiming to understand. The fact was: things jutted, got in the way. Malfred understood this from her relations with her own furniture. Her body was bruised in a score of places where her furniture had attacked it, and though she was too wise and experienced to be angry with it, or show violence against it in retaliation, it disturbed her not to have a clear pathway in rooms. But travel in rooms presented little difficulty compared with the desperation of trying to move about the earth, the towns, the cities, country places where thorns lay in wait: thorns, bidibids, paspallum (Malfred thought of "paspallum" with a new pride of possession, for it was an "up north" grass, something she had been told about "down south," and she had to confess to herself that the first time paspallum shed its sooty stain on the hem of her skirt she had recognized the moment as an occasion: a kind of "up north" blooding; an initiation.) Anything that hindered progress up, down, along the earth could be resented and attacked, particularly if you were young and had not yet learned to see or having been born with sight had not been taught to see. The mass of things was so illusive. It was little wonder that the "youths" spent their time smashing milk bottles when the things sat on gateposts, outside fences, in such idiotic milk-bottleness, taking up space and air, blocking the view. . . .

Malfred lay rigid in the darkness. In spite of the horror in the sudden withdrawal of the light she felt a maternal flow of excuses for possible louts who teased and tricked the middle aged, elderly and solitary. She did not quite know how to deal with the guilt she felt for having tricked the seeing of so many children. Yet had she tricked them? At the age they came to her, had they not already lost the original vision, the primitive view? Was it not merely part of their natural development to begin in light and move towards darkness? People had to be protected from living; living was a war that needed all the defenses one could gather, and what more useful, more satisfying defense was there than a restriction, distortion of the view? Had any real harm been done in teaching, commanding hundreds of children to draw fire shovels and the shadows of fire shovels? Had it not been merely a trimming of the view to fit the environment, a lesson in adaptation; and was not Adaptability another of the new Gods?

She suddenly spoke aloud. Her voice sounded strangely high-pitched. She hoped that she might be heard and her plea answered.

"Would you mind turning on my light, please?"

She felt that she sounded very polite, almost deferential. The house stayed in darkness. She could no longer hear the breathing and the whispering. She cleared her throat.

"I say."

Following this mild reprimand, she paused.

"I say!" she repeated. "Would you mind turning on my light, please?"

Again there was no answer to her plea. She groped for her torch. It was shockproof, waterproof, encased in rubber; she knew a flash of comfort to think that through earthquake, rain, lightning, thunder, her torch was guaranteed to keep its light. The light curved, mellow, upon the ceiling, directing itself upon the wound where the light fitting had been. Malfred shuddered at the dark-brown, bakelite hole in the ceiling. It reminded her of something she had witnessed when her mother was in the hospital. There had been a woman in the next bed, and for some reason, or as it may happen in hospitals, the woman was being attended to during visiting hours. Beyond the geraniums, the box of assorted centers, her mother, and the half-drawn patterned screen, Malfred saw with horror the woman lying with her body exposed, and on her lower right side there was a small, dark red hole with raw edges, as if something had been torn from the woman's body. At first, besides horror, Malfred felt anger and envy that the woman should have an extra, as it were, illegitimate hole in her body. What right had she? The holes of the body were so carefully counted and tended, and at death were given the last lingering attention . . . a triumphant, determined sealing. . . . And then the nurse was adjusting over the hole a polythene bag, about eight inches by six, perhaps smaller, like the bag in which handkerchiefs are kept, or sandwiches for a picnic lunch. . . .

The nurse suddenly turned and rattled the curtains swiftly along their railing, enclosing her with her patient, while Malfred turned to her mother and found, at her request, the orange liquid center, third in the middle row (to the left), withdrew it, unwrapped the crimson silver paper, and popped the chocolate into her mother's mouth.

She switched off the torch, then switched it on again, directing it towards the curtains on the window in front of the house. It was no use. She was only making herself a target, drawing attention to herself. It was terrible to be without light; it made one feel so powerless. Matches, torches, candles were no use; it had to be immediate swelling light that chased the shadows into the corners, that showed every object in the room; it had to be *electric* light.

"Please! Would you mind, please?"

There was no answer. The knocking had stopped, for the time being. She twitched her body to shake off its rigidity, as if it had fallen, like drops of rain, on her limbs. She crept from the bed, tiptoed into the sitting room to the front door, making sure that she did not stand directly in front of the glass panel; then with a bold movement that made her gasp for breath she opened the door, holding her body well back from the porch, trying to get her breath for the next step, and courage, too; in another swift move she was out the door, reaching up to unlatch the meter box, groping for the fat switch, pressing her thumb on it, then she turned, clinging to the door handle, using it to draw herself back to the house. She could scarcely breathe; her breath came ruggedly, painfully, yet, once she had opened the door and looked out and had the light behind her, she was not as frightened as before, and even though she still gasped for breath, she was bold enough now to take a step out of the porchway and peer around the corner of the house. She fancied she saw a figure darting away: it looked like someone young, perhaps a girl with a scarf of some flimsy material over her head. Then she thought she must have imagined it, for there was no one.

"Noni," she called sharply. "Noni!"

How ridiculous! Of all her pupils in all her years of teaching Art Noni had drawn the best fire shovels, the best distances, mountains, snow storms, apples (one side rosy, one side green, like the apples offered by the witch to Snow White), and Noni's shading had made Malfred sing her praises in the classroom and the staffroom and the Art Society meetings. Why? What had been the use?

"Noni," she called again.

Oh, it was not Noni, it was not anyone she knew. Hadn't it been the figure of a man, an old man?

Malfred groaned, and called out to the flax bushes and the manuka brush and the sea and the wind that had gone away, "I'll get the police to you. I'll get the police!"

Hurriedly now, she went inside and shut the front door. It was good to have the light again. She inspected the alcove critically. Yes; it had been a kitchen at some time. The taps had been wrenched from the wall. What had the carrier said when he brought her luggage and looked around the sitting room?

"I tell you it needs redecorating."

What did he mean? Why were people always wanting to "redecorate?" Next to motor mowing, it seemed to be the climax of everyone's weekend. Yet had not she, too, in a way, set about "redecorating" in beginning a new way of life? Though she was not so sure now that it *was* new; perhaps she would be like one of those plants that put out a shoot at a distance from the parent plant, yet because of the distance they do not blossom as other than what they have always been; they do not change.

In the reply to the carrier she had said timidly, "Do you think so?"

"I know pretty well every house on this island. I've been in them all."

So that was what the carrier had said to her. It puzzled her that at this time, with prowlers around, she should be making an effort to remember.

Then, putting her hand over her left breast, in a melodramatic gesture, and with her face white and her limbs trembling she crept back to bed. Thank God for the light, she thought. Thank God for the light. The carrier had said that the old woman had died alone in the house. She had replied that it did not trouble her very much to think of it, that anyone would want the house for the view alone. The View. The View. Another God to worship. People on a hill, the panoramic people. Panoramania. Why?

She had just climbed into bed, adjusted her pillow, drawn the blankets up to her neck and set her body in humble coffin position, when the house was once again in darkness. They—she bestowed the universally overpowering pronoun of unfairness, resentment, fear, power—"they" had come back, they were determined to besiege her, to stay all night; they would break into the house; perhaps they would murder her, batter her over the head, as they do with middle-aged women living alone; they would have a blunt instrument, a hammer.

Determinedly, she tried to keep calm. In a slow, moderately loud voice, directing her remarks to the curtain of the front window she said, "I'll get the police if you don't turn on my light. I know you're there. I've seen you. Will you please turn on my light?"

There was no sound from outside.

Then suddenly she had an inspiration. The telephone in the sitting room! She could creep to it and pretend to phone the police—or someone—for help. She would make a great noise about dialing. She would talk in a loud voice so that whoever was outside would hear and know that the police were being sent for.

She paused in thinking of her inspiration to sigh at her wishful plural—the police; they. She knew, and whoever was outside must know, that there was one policeman only on the island, and he was likely to be asleep or away. All the same, she might be able to frighten the prowler with her phone call. Prowlers, she supposed, were human beings subject to fear?

She tiptoed again to the sitting room and switched on the light above the telephone shelf. Nothing happened. Of course! Once again she braved the front door, the meter box, hastily turned on the switch, hurried back into the room, this time slamming the door behind her. The light above the telephone showed not too brightly—forty watt only—and would not give the prowler light enough to see through the glass panel into the room. She sat on the sofa bed by the window, took the telephone from the shelf and put it down beside her. She left her fingerprints in the dust on it, and wrinkling her nose she flicked a piece of mousedirt from one of the grooves. She picked up the receiver, making as much noise as she could, she blew the dust from the earpiece of the phone, and leaned it against her ear. She rested her finger on the 9 in the dial. How ridiculous, she thought. Dial 999 London Metropolitan Police, Fire Brigade, Ambulance. I complain of having news gurgled underwater from the BBC, and here I dial 999 in case of emergency!

She had dreamed once of going to London. So many of the teachers of her generation had gone there, attending ceremonies in Westminster Abbey, garden parties at Buckingham Palace, Shakespeare Festivals at Stratford-On-Avon, and had returned with postcards, photos, and travelers' tales that might seem unbelievable but could not be questioned by stay-at-homes who had never been out of their own country. Yet the miraculous change that should have overcome the travelers had been absent. Miss Hetherby, the Senior History mistress, was the same old carp she had always been, and after a few months when her travelers' tales and comparisons had run dry few would have known that she'd ever been anywhere, let alone overseas and to London. She taught history in the same way as before. She moved happily and peacefully from life in London to the same Kings and Queens whose graves she had walked on without having found out whether the good were so good or the bad were so bad. She returned to the Maori Wars and the shortcomings of Mr. Busby, shutting the door carefully behind her, as if her overseas journey had been too draughty a venture.

And then there had been Miss Float who went on exchange to Fort William, Scotland, and came back saying, "Aye, Aye, Aye." Yet all her traveling had not given her the courage to read aloud to her fourth form the whole of *To a Daisy*. She still skipped, with blushes, the verse:

Such is the fate of man or maid
Sweet floweret of the rural shade,
By love's simplicity betrayed.

Miss Float went away a prim kindly soul; she returned, apparently unextended, as if she had traveled in her own encircling tube of being which is, after all, the way that no one can avoid traveling. Yet perhaps her journey had given her the prerogative of inventing an interesting story for her rocking-chair retirement. Sometimes a gleam came into her eye, and the curiosity of the staff was aroused. Perhaps, they said amongst themselves . . . Perhaps, after all . . .

Miss Float, with the spotted blouse. Elizabeth Float. Oh the madness of it all, Malfred said to herself, dialing 999 London Metropolitan Police, Fire, Ambulance.

Her voice was loud and harsh. There was a phrase of music swirling about her ears and it would not go away; it had been salvaged from the silence, the night-silence that tries murderously to stop wood from talking, leaves from rustling, tin roofs from knuckle-cracking; the frightful, domineering silence of night. Now that the wind and the sea were hushed, the night had control of everything but the human body. It was Malfred's intentness of listening that drew the phrase out of the silence; it came naturally like a bud opening into the sun; but it was the phrase from a radio commercial, an advertisement for a deodorant, "Instant Banish," that Malfred had heard when she switched on the radio.

"Instant Banish" How I Need You,
Quick Sweet Fresh
Quick Sweet Fresh.

It would not go away. It stayed with its mocking vulgarity: Quick Sweet Fresh Quick Sweet Fresh.

Malfred spoke louder, to exterminate the sudden parasite.

"Oh. May I speak to the Constable, please? Oh, is that you, Constable? Yes. I'm sorry to trouble you. There's a prowler.

Malfred Signal. Yes. I moved in here some days ago. Yes. The white house on the hill. There's a prowler. Someone outside. You'll come at once? Thank you. Thank you."

Now that she had the telephone receiver in her hand she could not bear to part with it, she wanted to speak into it, in a loud confident voice, but what could she say, other than "Thank you Constable, I'm very grateful. Yes, at once. Thank you." Yet she felt that whoever was outside had stopped to listen, had fallen under the spell of her call for help, and that as soon as she put the receiver down he (she had decided the prowler was a man) would again switch off her light and begin knocking on the door. She clung to the receiver. Quick Sweet Fresh. Quick Sweet Fresh. Quick Sweet Fresh. What could she say?

"Thank you, Constable. I'm glad you're coming at once. Two minutes, you said. With reinforcements. Good. Thank you." She replaced the receiver, still clinging to it, dialed a fictitious number, lifted the receiver, and began to speak.

"Oh, hello. I noticed you had the phone. I'm your new neighbor, two houses away. The white house on the hill. With the old weather vane. I look out over the gulf and the islands and perhaps the distant coast of South America. I've noticed you in your garden, weeding the lettuces. And getting the milk from the box at the gate. And your letters. The postman comes every day—isn't it a marvel, I thought he'd come only on Mondays, Wednesdays and Fridays or Tuesdays, Thursdays and Saturdays. I was told he would. There's a prowler outside my house, a burglar. The police are coming immediately. I'm glad I've got the phone. I noticed you had the phone. I saw the kingfishers sitting on your telephone wires, and I traced the lines to your house and I said to myself, They're on the phone, I'm glad they're on the phone and I'm glad I'm on the phone. Isn't it ridiculous the way I've been chatting to you while I'm waiting for the police to come to arrest the prowler, and I haven't let you get a word in edgeways. Yes, of course. Yes. I'm so glad your husband can come to help the police. No, I've not been very much frightened, I know the police can handle the affair. I believe I hear their car now. No, I'm sorry I shan't be visiting much while I'm here, though afternoon tea would indeed be a pleasure."

Down, down, she was rolling down the steps of all the platitudes she had heard of, those wide white stone steps kissed by pilgrims, even those from Matuatangi with its wool stores, rabbitskin factory, schools, teachers of Art who would take their useful shining black fire shovels to Hell with them.

"Yes, it would be a pleasure to come to tea. Pavlova cake, meringues, melting moments. Yes, it's the police now, I'm sure it is. I can hear the car. They've brought a reinforcement of neighbors. Everyone has been so kind to me during my short stay. Yes, I'm sure I'm going to like Karemoana. I've a lemon tree in my garden, and a fig tree, and big subtropical flowers, flame colored; a pine tree too huge and heavy for comfort, dropping split cones in the dry grass; a flax bush—three flax bushes crackling in the wind the black dried flowers jutting like beaks into the sky; and there are flowers that I don't know the name of because I've lived down south all my life, and I'm not used to the tough-leaved, subtropical plants that hide all promise and hint of their delicate flowers; though we had passionfruit down south, our local member of Parliament had a passionfruit vine on the verandah of his house. The skin of passionfruit is dark blue-gray, wrinkled, leathery, like the skin and corns of an old woman's foot, but once you break the skin of the fruit your tongue darts inside like a snake's tongue to slip between the seed and the pulp and juice; oh I know passionfruit, I've always known it, coming from down south as I do, but fijoas are new to me, like sandseeds, and guavas, like strawberries, and figs growing in one's own garden, and pawpaws and Chinese gooseberries belly to the earth; and then there are the orange trees and the lemon trees . . .

"Yes, the police are almost here, yes. That's the car climbing the hill now. Yes, I suppose you would be able to hear it from your house. I think I can hear all the cars on the island when they change gears. Retired, yes. I suppose you guessed; most people do. We former schoolteachers have an unfortunate way of revealing ourselves. Oh? That's kind of you to say so. Perhaps it *is* fortunate. I taught Art for nearly thirty years. I showed primary and secondary pupils how to draw fire shovels; garden shovels, too, and spades; yes, coal scuttles, too, and fire tongs; jugs, teapots, boats with sails; tables; chairs—no, no, the chairs never burst into flames, not in my time; dishes of fruit, fruit of temperate climates, not subtropical fruit. We drew maps, too; Bights and Bays, Mountains and Lakes, Cities. Shading was so important. I trembled with love of shading. Shadows falling like rain. Oh? The shadow of a fire shovel did seem to be more important than the shovel itself. . . .

"Yes, the police are here now. I think they're here. They've brought reinforcements from the city, in a police launch, that blue launch you see moored at the steps over in Auckland; yes, they're equipped with radio, they can fly through the water. It's terrible to be middle-aged and alone when it's night and there's a prowler outside and your blood makes a rushing noise like a river, and there's singing in your ears and whispering, whispering; then some kind of filament encircles your gray hair, like a halo; there's a burning of manganese. No, thank you all the same, I intend to be very busy in my new life here, I've so much work to do, I'm spring-cleaning the room "two inches behind the eyes" and I'm not practiced in domesticity, not on my own accord; there was my mother, of course . . . I'm learning to see for the first time in my life—blind? oh no!—it sounds ridiculous, perhaps you will laugh; I don't expect people to understand; understanding's a subject to be studied, to be trained in, like shading. I'm going to stare, to see. It's no crime. Oh no, I'll be very busy. I never cared for the Women's Institute anyway. The Library Committee? I must apologize. The Karemoana Spinners and Weavers? It's so kind of you but I must refuse. A silver cup, you say, for the best original play? I've never written a play, I'm not of a literary turn of mind. Did you? Well many schoolteachers do when they retire. Everyone seems to now, on retirement. Yes, it helps if you're a General or have known one or two Prime Ministers, and in this country if your people came over in the *first* ships—after a certain date you're nobody at all, you can't even belong to the Early Settlers' Society. Yes, I paint. No, not bicycles. Or pieces of bedsteads and borer-riddled wardrobes, though they *are* the spare parts of our life, just as the strands of human hair, leftover cotton and wool threads were the spare materials for the early settlers, for the women to make their pictures of wool and hair; the action painters are not very far from the pursuits of an afternoon at the Women's Club! Oh no, I shall be keeping myself to myself. At my age one has to make very careful apportioning of one's time, especially if one has spent most of one's life wasting it. Yes, this is the police now. Your husband is with them. The spirit of neighborliness is not lost. They must have brought all available men."

The receiver was hot and sticky where her hand clung to it. It was a gesture of surrender at last to replace it in its cradle, to put the phone back on the shelf, to admit that as the light was once again turned off and the grass swished again as with the movements of footsteps, and the knocking sounded with renewed force, that there was no car full of policemen and neighbors, the phone was attached to a useless length of cord, connected to nothing, and she was alone again, besieged in the dark with no help.

·14·

SHE SAW HERSELF WALKING on the island. The light was so clear, a bright gold. There was so much more room in the sky for it to flow here, up north; and beyond it the clouds drifted, small, round, white, like featherweight pebbles; then a goldrush came, the light and the pebbles were snapped up, there was subtropical darkness, a most cruel island darkness that wedged in the people beside the plants, animals, insects, while the sea stood guard.

She walked on the island, up and down the roads that were thin black lines on the map but under the feet they were obstacles of clay, metal, potholes filled with water after the last rain, while on each side the starry white manuka bushes swayed in the wind, and flowers new to Malfred were budding crimson and yellow. She walked again to the village nearest the wharf— Kare. She passed two bulldozers sleeping in the sun, their clay-filled teeth half-sunk in the earth; beside them a pile of gorse ready for a bonfire, stiff-skirted, bunched, with tough thin stems like the legs of old fowls, grasped the air with their thorn-claws. The section had been cleared. On either side, the gorse and manuka still crowded the space, but here the path had been made clear for building, the section was neat, empty, level. Malfred stared, trying to *see*, at the baches, the gardens and their trees and flowers. She tried not to let one word come into her mind when she met the few people coming from or going to Kare with their shopping baskets and their walking sticks and their limps. *Decrepit* was the word. Am I like that too? she wondered. Have I really come here like a worn-out elephant or those animals that hide when they are lame or sick, to die? The island is ful of aging men and women, or those whose thoughts are on age, who have escaped to retire, that is, to await the metamorphosis of retirement as if it were an inevitable phase in the human life-cycle. I am one of those. We're a small, pitiful band of islanders who, tired of setting up the human walls that generation builds between generation, have come to Karemoana, asking the sea to be our wall; there's no cost of maintenance here; inexhaustible, self-repairing, lovely wall of water; the paint never washes out of the sea.

All up and down our country, up north, down south, people are needing paint, needing it for themselves and for their houses. I've never been overseas. I never got to London like Miss Hetherby and Miss Float; or Miss Cartright who went to Fiji and came back with Matuavosa. I've been here only, up north, yet I think that our country out of all the countries in the world needs paint most desperately. In other countries so many of the houses are stone; and stone is stone with its own skin, but here we have asked the trees to share our secret lives, to spy on us as inside, outside walls, and when the fear seizes us we know we must paint those walls. Paper, paint. In bright colors. To keep the storm out, to keep the storm in. We're painting, painting ourselves and our houses. When I visited Graham and Fernie in Christchurch they were painting their house and their garden shed was full of tins of Gloss, Enamel, Turpentine, paint and paintbrushes; and everywhere there were houses being pulled down and put up and there was paint being burned off with blow torches and layered on with big, soft brushes; and the only time the wood had a chance to be heard, whatever speech it cared to make, was at night, in the dark; and then it told of its life, of the colors it had known, of all the wooden buildings up north down south. The color of boards, dry and wet, with nests of knot-holes and dark stains where the rain decided to stay; the railway-color, hut-color, and house-color; the color of the old houses that no one wanted any more to paint; the lace-like verandahs weathered gray with thin white lines like cotton thread set in the boards; or perhaps they were white spider webs; the new houses with their brazen colors—bright blues, reds, greens; you name it, their drunken spectrum said to them; you name it. . . .

When I spoke of coming here and buying my home, they told me with a note of urgency in their voices, "Every five years you'll have to paint. You can't leave it longer. Every five years you must paint your house. Paint preserves, maintains, seals, is a defense you can never do without. It's all right if your house is made of *stone*—oh yes, it's all right with stone, but *wood!*"

I suppose I must paint my house, as I've painted my face all these years; only this lovely wall of sea is self-restoring. And then I'll return to that other kind of painting that is not written into a State Advances Loan Contract; and when I paint my kind of painting I shan't be sealing my house from storm—or do I deceive myself in thinking this?

She passed the decrepit people. They were so eager to speak to her, as if they had been separated a long time from their kind. They asked after the city, the mainland. Did she work there? Would she be going there and back in the hydrofoil? Had she traveled in the hydrofoil? It was *new.* The word *new* was spoken in a strange wondering tone. There was a thin veil of alarm in their eyes when she said, No she did not work in the city, she had retired. They began to talk, then, of the doctor, the only one on the island; they said how kind he was, how well he understood their ailments.

"You are ill?" Malfred asked an elderly man who had been taking his daily walk to and from the beach.

He replied, "Most of us here have something the matter. But we don't get the green vegetables. Not here."

Several of the women spoke of the vegetables.

"There's not the green vegetables," they said. And because Malfred had come recently to the island and would presumably have had her share there (or more than her share!) of green vegetables, they looked accusingly at her.

"But don't you even have small gardens?"

"There's no room, with all the sewage. There's no place in the country so full of sewage. But it's not that. The green vegetables are just not available."

They had fixed in their mind an image of mountains of green vegetables more precious to them than mountains of gold. It was useless for Malfred to try to peel or tear it away by explaining to them that their longing might be for youth, the green growth and health of youth.

"The cabbage leaves are *yeller,*" the old man said; his complaint was a cry of despair.

"And what if you get ill, here on the island?"

They wanted the wall; at the same time they wanted to tear it down. And when they looked more closely at Malfred and saw the lines of middle age in her face, and the gray in her hair, they knew she was one of them, that if in time she didn't worry because the vegetables were yellow and not green, and the hospital had to be reached by ship, then she would worry about other affairs, mixing her own concerns with those of the island. Perhaps, buying last summer's chocolate, she would find maggots inside it; or weevils in the walnuts. She would learn to recognize her own complaint; but always the loudest complaint would be against the sea, the warder, set there to stop her from escaping.

"The cabbage leaves are all yeller!" the old man said, raising his stick to strike. Malfred saw, in the darkness, that the old man was her father.

"But you never grew old," she said. "You were the young lawyer, the schoolmaster, the mountaineer, the much-loved mild man who named the peaks and explored beyond the Southern Lakes."

The room spoke, the wood in the walls spoke. The room was dark. The knocking went on and on and no help came.

·15·

AND NOW SHE WAS stopping at the restaurant on the corner for a cup of coffee and a sandwich or biscuit. There were steaming pies under glass on the counter and she swayed as if hypnotized, towards them.

"Like a hot pie? Mince and peas?"

She nodded. Yes, she would like a hot pie. Fatty, indigestible, but to be surrounded by the smell brought a temptation that was hard to resist, and as her total temptations were few, she felt, or was persuaded to feel, that she ought to surrender to it. Go on, pamper yourself.

She sat, coping, at a narrow table.

"You're from England?" the proprietor asked.

She almost gave way to that temptation, too. Once before when she had done so she had received the sharp reprimand—she had complained about a price—"Why don't you go back to your own country?" She knew, though, that the question was a random one, put out for any foreigner, whether English or Scottish or Irish, or—South Island; from anywhere but Karemoana.

She shook her head. The proprietor tried again.

"From the south? You've come over for the day? It's a popular spot in good weather."

Someone else had asked her the same question before. Have you come over for the day? The people of the island were reluctant to admit new settlers.

"No, I'm living here."

"Oh?"

"The white house on the hill."

The proprietor looked alarmed, then sympathetic, and lifted the glass bowl up and down over the plate of sandwiches and buttered scones, letting in a fly, and then, seeing that Malfred saw the fly, looking more alarmed.

"Yes," he said. "On the island you never know where a fly has been before it comes in here. They say we won't have water laid on for at least ten years. I like it here. Every time I go over to the mainland I can't stick it. So you're living in the cottage on the hill. An elderly woman lived there. Retired from teaching. She used to come here to order her firewood. I'd say it's a peaceful place to retire to. With the hydrofoil, we're supposed to be going ahead."

He gazed out the door, over the almost deserted road, to the bay and the dark mass of pohutukawas edging the cliff.

"We're going ahead all right."

"Do you want to go ahead?"

He shrugged. "Trade's bad in the winter months. But there's the weekends. Folks from the city come over for picnics. And there's the summer. We get the louts then."

He paused, looked at her, and spoke in a warning tone. "There's an element here, you know, a bad element. It comes here and yet it's here to start with. You might meet it."

He spoke of the "element" as if it were a kind of weather, a traveling isobar that happened, that was no one's responsibility. "Windows broken, baches burned down, gardens trampled, plants uprooted."

Malfred condemned herself for supposing that he was going to add the usual pearl to the string—"teenagers." He didn't. "You might meet the element," he said again. "The other woman did —the retired teacher."

Malfred finished her pie and escaped from the confining table and seat, noting, with a feeling of depression that was not entirely post-pastry that whoever had built the restaurant had followed the modern principle of making seats so uncomfortable that the diners would eat quickly, then make way for the rest of the hungry holiday crowd.

"I suppose you have more than you can cope with in summer?"

"The whole family helps in summer. Even then we're rushed off our feet."

It was no use trying to suggest to him a summer and winter method of seating. Outside, in the roughly metaled street, the same few people limped, hobbled, walked slowly along. Malfred looked out at them with an expression of sympathy. The proprietor, noticing this, was about to become confiding and philosophical when Malfred did something that was apparently unforgivable: she sneezed.

Drawing back, his hand now clamped firmly on the handle of the glass bowl as if to stop the sandwiches from escaping, or perhaps to protect them from foreign contamination that was more dreadful than a neighborly island fly, the proprietor said slowly, suspiciously, "There's flu on the mainland. We don't want it here. There's something to be said for screening visitors to the island. Some say there should be passports, visas, health certificates. Oh no," he said hastily. "I don't mean you, not the likes of you."

But when Malfred sneezed a second time she knew by his look of alarm that he did mean her.

"No, you live here."

Malfred thought he was going to suggest a system of quarantine.

She decided to adopt the "intelligent" approach. "If Karemoana is so isolated that it doesn't get flu, it may be in danger. You know how these island communities are struck down because they've lost their natural immunity through contact with disease. Look at Pitcairn."

"Pitcairn?"

The proprietor relaxed. "I've always wanted to go there on a visit. They're different, of course. I believe they're dying out."

"They're not different," Malfred said sternly. "They're vulnerable. Karemoana is vulnerable. They're vulnerable because they're in prison."

"I say! If you're going to talk like that you won't like living here."

He gave the familiar challenge then, varied to fit the circumstances. "Why don't you go back to the South Island?"

The peas had been bright green with spots of yellow in them, the mince had been heavily floured. Malfred felt ashamed and uncomfortable at having given way to the odor of a hot pie. How many times she had stood in the staffroom and joined the declamation about the little shop at the corner that was ruining the girls' teeth, digestion and general health with its hot pies, ice creams and sweets! Why, in Malfred's day—she thought suddenly, with nostalgia, of "her day"; she saw an image of it as a magic carpet suspended over the world, with her sitting on it waiting for it to take her wherever she wanted to go; why had everything been so limited? It had not been her "day" but the carpet that had been limited in its journeying. It had been her own dreams, her own view; she had been bound by the outlines of objects, the prison of shape; a flower vase out of proportion had sent her into a rage; a house with bulging walls; a crooked highway; a coal scuttle with a pencil dent in its side, had depressed and worried her. Even, high in the sky, with the promise of endless fulfillment of wishes, she had been bound by the rectangular shape of the carpet, by the definite edges of her dreamed-of "day."

"Well, why don't you go back?"

She smiled.

"In my day," she thought, "a hot pie was a crime."

She spoke aloud. "But it's true! Where did they exile Napoleon?"

"Elba," the proprietor said swiftly. "The island of Elba." Malfred did not know that when she asked the question he heard in his mind the tantalizing voice, "And now for the glamour prize, the twenty-three-inch television set with armchair control, special filter, table specially shod; also the motor mower with inset magic blades, the ten-cubic-foot deep freeze . . ."

"Right." Malfred spoke in her former tone of a schoolteacher acknowledging the right answer to a question. "And where do they put the alcoholics, epileptics, criminals, lepers, anyone who, they think, I mean society thinks, is best out of sight?"

Malfred wished she had not said this. The proprietor looked indignant. "If you're suggesting . . ."

"I'm not, of course. But there must be some kind of traffic between us and the mainland. . . ."

"Oh there's the traffic, the ferries, the hydrofoil . . ."

Another customer came into the shop. The proprietor called out, "G'day, Bob."

Bob came slowly up to the counter. He was a small, wiry man in a checked shirt. His face was sun-tanned, wrinkled. He drew an object from his pocket.

"The Board is at it again, Harry. How's the voltage this morning?"

Without waiting for an answer he went behind the counter to the three-pin plug, unplugged the pie-warmer, inserted his voltage measurer, and after a few moments gave an exclamation of triumph. "Yes, they're at it again. It's dropped!"

He returned the voltage measurer to his pocket, and going towards the door called back over his shoulder, "Can't stop for a cup of tea. Save me a *Record* will you? I suspected the Board was up to something."

Malfred tried to pretend she had not heard this mysterious exchange, for it had seemed to be a domestic matter which as a newcomer she was not yet entitled to share. She felt embarrassed.

The restaurant proprietor however showed no embarrassment.

"The Board's been monkeying around again," he said simply. "Or, so it seems. Do you want me to save any newspapers . . . a *Record?* It comes out once a fortnight. Edited by some chap on the mainland."

Prison, lepers were forgotten.

"I haven't decided yet," Malfred said. "I'll let you know."

"The dailies come late from the mainland. We have to kowtow to the mainland."

Did she detect a note of—pride, gratitude—in his voice as he complained of having to kowtow? The comforts of dependence were lasting, deep, necessary. The proprietor was yet bound to the mainland by the weekly bundle of women's journals with their lace-knitting patterns, *Best Bets, Sports Flash,* and the daily mainland papers that arrived tied together by thin wire. Hadn't she seen one of the shopkeepers along the high road trying to get at the papers, having her fingers torn by the wire while the little group of people from the neighboring baches surrounded her, ready to pounce on the revealed news, or on her, if she did not manage to untangle the wire more quickly?

Oh, they were hungry for news! She had seen it in their eyes, in the way they looked about them when they walked along the street, searching the air, the sky, the sea, for news; and they found it, or if they did not find it, they invented it. A whale had passed the island, the afternoon before. No, a school of whales. The hydrofoil had broken down. Someone had been rushed by plane to hospital on the mainland. Speaking confidentially . . .

Malfred was waiting for news, too. She was not in prison; oh

no, she was not bound hand and foot to a city, with thin wire
that tore her flesh; but she knew that something in her mind still
waited to hear how her mother had "managed" at the moment of
death. She could see her mother, long before the days of her
illness, sitting at the dinner table, looking proudly at the tablecloth and the silver and the dinner service; and proudly, too, at
her three children, grown up, intelligent, loyal; and then turning
to look at their father (it was not long after he left the Law
Office to teach), addressing her remarks to him, telling how she
had "managed" every unruly moment during the day, presenting
the time as threatening, rebellious, until she had put out a calm
hand, as if to subdue a wild animal, to "manage" it. Malfred
could not remember that her mother had ever confessed to not
having managed, though she suspected that moments and hours
had often overcome her.

After their father's death, when Lucy was still at school, then
had been the time when the decision was made for Lucy to leave.
Malfred was a qualified teacher by then; the fire shovels were
well in command of her life; and she dared not look beyond the
water colors of the Canterbury Plains and other local scenes for
fear she might see something not quite in order. She was fond of
Lucy. She remembered looking down from the platform of the
Assembly Hall at the fourth-former, flushed with intermittent
weeping at the funeral, and now flushed with the personal prestige of bereavement. The other girls looked at her with envy. Her
father was dead. He had been a schoolteacher at the Boys' High.
There had been a special service for him. The Signals were
clever, interesting, rich; they owned half of Matuatangi. How
much they really owned was evident, but not accepted by Lucy's
romantic fellow pupils, when Mrs. Signal, in an attempt to keep

up her record of "managing," suggested that Lucy leave school to get a job. A job. It was unheard of. Training College, University, teaching, medicine, anything professional; perhaps nursing—yes; but a job! The idea of ordinary work was a blow—at least it was a blow to everyone but Lucy whom the teachers described to one another, in reports, and to Lucy herself, as "scatty." "Lacks concentration." "Could do better." "Shows little interest in her work. . . ."

Lucy was a confused, forgetful schoolgirl of the kind that suffers most keenly under algebraic and geometric rules; no one seemed ever to understand the elbowing tyranny of triangles, the seeds of Hell enclosed in the jovial, well-fed circles; as for the other shapes with their strange names reminiscent of the names of extinct animals and birds, one could only run from them and hide; and this Lucy did, when the family affairs were considered and there was found to be not enough money, even with the contributions made by Graham and Malfred. Poor Lucy ran in a blind panic from the triangles and circles and the blots to the department just inside the door, on the right, of Fleet and Milligan, Drapers, in the Main Street of Matuatangi; and there she sold domes, buttons, elastic, ribbons, lace, haberdashery. Fleet and Milligan, one of the oldest established firms in Matuatangi, had made their building in the guise of a temple. Lucy's department was bounded by two plaster pillars that served as decoration, reminders of aristocracy and wealth, and as links to hold the wire that led to the office from each department, and along which Lucy shot, as from mountain to mountain, the brass containers full of cash and crumpled, smudged dockets. Going to the shop one day to buy hooks and eyes, Malfred was saddened to see that the tiny, black, twinned notions, the cards of elastic, lace, ribbon, seemed to be exerting the same kind of tyranny as the triangles, circles, pentagons, tetrahedrons and cylinders had done. Malfred felt sad to see Lucy's evident confused dealings with the "world."

Now there had been, at one time, a piece of rage inside Malfred—a ragged shape that splintered like steel wool, that was useful for removing stains of emotion and experience, though it left in the process a gritty deposit of rust—that hurt most when it was not in use. Malfred had a clear understanding of its origin. Why, she had wondered again and again, when Lucy was not able to cope with the affairs of the world, had she married so early, so successfully, getting love and money and in return scattering goodness-knew what muddle of notions gathered from her special "department?" Malfred learned in time not to dwell on the fairness or unfairness of fortune, though her brief past preoccupation with it had left on each side of her mouth two prim, bitter lines that showed when her heart was too full to express what it felt and her body took over to be rid of some of the urgent speech. These bitter lines never lost an opportunity to say, "Life's been unfair, unfair, unfair"—even when Malfred had, or thought she had, long forgotten her bitterness. The repetition acted as its own advertisement. People who knew Malfred, who had seen her in moments of tension, would think, with pity or with gratitude for their own escape: Life's been unfair to her; they had received the message; it was a message buried in her skin as the marauding footprint of an extinct animal was buried in stone.

Here, now, Malfred longed for details of her mother's management of death. She wanted the news to come out, the secret to be heard. She knew that she had been her mother's support during her illness, and she had been proud of her acquired skill in dealing with a long illness, proud too that she had never used her mother's illness as an excuse or complaint; she had kept it apart from her personal life. But how she longed to know, to know, that in some way her mother had at last *not* been able to manage: Would she be saying, "Malfred, do spare a minute to help! I need your help to die. Malfred. Mally, Mally!" She was screaming now. Malfred felt her heart beating fast with relief, with fear, too. So the intruder outside was not her father seeking shelter on one of his mountain expeditions, nor her sister Lucy running in fear from the pursuing circles and triangles, the clear-eyed isosceles, the squint-eyed scalene . . . it was her mother. Death had come to her, had taken her warm life from her as if it had been a fur coat growing on her body, and now she was naked, plucked, shapeless—oh, the beautiful unguessed shape of experience; she was an infant clamoring to get in—or out; she was admitting at last that she was afraid, lonely, overwhelmed; that the last event of her life had swarmed upon her as with the force of an army on an unprepared city. The attack that she had feared for so many years had been too sudden for her to rally her "managing" ability.

"I'll not let her in," Malfred thought. "I loved her. I spent years of my life looking after her, while Graham and Fernie and Lucy and Roland were so free that they had to anchor their limbs to their double beds to prevent themselves from flying away. I loved mother but I'll not let her in because her life and her death have helped to make me a walking cliché. Few realize the danger threatening a life that has become a walking cliché. One is judged more often, because judgments come more easily. In situations where judgments are crucial there is little hope of fair play; even my rare visits to the doctor bring the expected remark—'You spent some years looking after your mother, didn't you?' and the habitual, not always spoken conclusion—'You're in pain because you've a grudge against the world because you feel you've wasted the best years of your life tending an invalid mother. . . .'

"With such tightly packed clichés attached to me," Malfred thought, "to me as the central cliché, there's little use trying to wedge into my spare judgment-free area even a speck or spark of truth. What should my life be like if a spark of truth were to fall and spread like wildfire? I should know such a satisfying conflagration of clichés! Yet, I should feel the cold once the fire had died, for it takes so long for the attitudes of other people to grow on one, and when they have grown thick and fast they do keep one warm in winter! Yet with all these judgments, I've become a kind of off-the-peg personality. I could be anyone. I could be the woman who died in this house, or the one who will follow when I die. I've come, with those retired people that walk the high roads of Karemoana to escape a derelict self by joining the derelict people. No matter what excuse I give to myself or to others, I came here to practice a new way of seeing; forgetting, for the moment, that I brought my used eyes with me. They have been trained so long ago that they find it hard to give up their old tricks, let alone learn new ones. If I opened the door now, if I answered my mother's plea to let her in from the storm or the dead, she would cause me to forget my problems of seeing. She would sit at that fireside in the sitting room, talking of the "olden" days, of her husband and his family, of her own family, her mother and father and children, the hopes she had for them, and the time in her life when she had to trim her hopes to fit the sudden shock of bereavement. Francis Henry Signal had not suffered a chronic illness. A passing devastation—flu, that no one has painted with its deserved emphasis of tragedy, carried him off. Not many citizens at his youthful age had accumulated so many named drinking fountains, had planted so many native trees, climbed so many mountains.

"And yet"—Malfred said to herself—"what I fear most, if I open the door to mother, would be her plea that I return 'down south.' She would say again and again that I was born and bred in the south and the south is my true home. She would use that expression 'in your bones,' knowing that I could not discount it, for my bones were composed of whatever came out of the Canterbury Plains and the lime-filled soil of Matuatangi, with an occasional 'imported' sediment—a handful of Christmas muscatels, paper lollies from England; surely some part of these found its way into my bones; and pineapples; other tropical fruit. . .

"I know that when my mother makes these demands upon my loyalties of place I'll concede that so much of the south found its way into my bones; that the special long bones of being that propel from here to there are made from alpine rock with scratches of snow on the surface, or old volcanic sediment; that I've been mixed in river basins, evened on plains, that my heart, like the magpies, has been several times 'up a gum tree'; that I've known the kind of erosion that puts on view what one had hoped was lost or forgotten; that I've had areas of myself thrown up in shock and not known at first how to deal with the vast, salt-sprinkled deserts where the South Pacific laps and a few long-legged sea birds wade, timidly, looking for places to nest. Were I ten, twenty, thirty years younger, I should listen to my mother's plea; even now I shall find it hard to resist. I remember that I've never known such a feeling of safety as I knew in Matuatangi when I woke each morning and knew that the school day, with its fire shovels, lay ahead; that my lessons were planned down to the last shadow. I knew which days I should prepare morning tea, supervise the playground, coach games after school. How can I ever explain to anyone my feeling of joy when I stood before my class and watched everyone busy with drawing or painting and knew that I had regretfully dispensed with the cliché comfort of the teaching profession—the discovery of genius—to replace it with shadows and with the calmer knowledge that no one in my classroom would ever 'burst into that silent sea.' It was the joy gained from doing what is looked on as a virtue; the virtuous joy of having faced facts; that in my classes I shone no lights in no windows. Had there been genius, even regarding the superior staying power of genius, it would not have survived in my classroom. I knew how to blot! How useful my shadows were! It is in revenge against me that, as evening and old age approach, the same shadows grow longer and thinner, as thin as the shadows of dragonflies; and the sky presses down upon the earth and upon my body—I feel it at the base of my neck; I must bow my head into the old-woman-praying or old-woman knitting position.

"No one has known, ever, the persistence, and now, the persecution, of shadows in my life. I'll let no one in. You can thrust at a shadow with a knife, but not cut it; you can stamp on it and not break it; you can push it and it will not move; but if it is part of a tree the wind may move it; you can encircle it with a boundary of chalk, but it will escape, and watching it grow or diminish, you are envious of its intimacy with light. There are stories of shadows that are stolen, that bleed, that are mislaid. Was there not, once upon a time, a young prince who was forced to live his entire life deprived of his shadow? Do the dead throw shadows when they knock, as Mother is knocking now, to get in?

"Can I escape her if I take my double-B pencil and return to my former ways of seeing, of making shade when the fire of looking is too fierce?

"Drawing master, sharpen this doubly-soft heart of lead, pencil-shape these dead?"

·16·

IN THE MIDST OF the dark and the waiting and the longing for the prowler to be identified, Malfred found herself thinking of summer at Karemoana. She had been told that at Christmas the pohutukawas "were a blaze" along the coast. She felt ashamed that she had never seen pohutukawa in blossom, though she remembered that when Miss Hetherby and Miss Float were overseas she had sent them Christmas cards showing pohutukawas in blossom. She could have chosen mud-pools, geysers, Maori maidens, or a Beautiful New Zealand Calendar, for all were on display in the stationer's, and everyone was buying them to send to friends overseas, and why should one buy other cards (Magi, etc.) when it was safer and more comforting to follow the crowd —in a discriminating way, of course? It had been Wilfred who explained to Malfred this aspect of "getting along" as he called it. And because, when one is in love, one can listen to the dullest theories advanced by the beloved and still think them new and worthy (though one may have already rejected them, in one's personal trials), Malfred had taken this philosophy on trust, had tried it (how changed it was, with his approval shining on it!), and after a few years of married life she might have been disenchanted enough to forget it, had not Wilfred's death bequeathed his theories to her in a form that until now had seemed permanent, embedded in surrounding clusters of those precious grief-stones and hope-stones that are indestructibly part of one's emotional geology.

Now, with the upheaval of her journey north to her new life and her new way of seeing, Malfred had (or dreamed she had) emerged to see the long-treasured theories, once jewels, in their new, true form, as barnacles. Her shame at not having known pohutukawas was not as deep as it would have been in the "old" days. Pohutukawas, geysers, Maori maidens—she knew none of these. Down south there had been few Maoris. She had learned about them at school—about the "good" and the "bad," the "friendly," the "hostile"; all in a legend of the Fire in the Fern, Mr. Busby, the cutting down of the Flagstaff. Lucy had a book of Maori fairy tales that Malfred had never been able to cope with, as she had with the Greek and Roman legends. Once or twice, in a burst of patriotism, she had asked the girls to illustrate a Maori legend—Rangi, Hinemoa, Maui. All except one girl— Lettice Bradley—had produced a painting that had no truth or conviction or foundation; as if the national history were too fragile to attract dreaming or the belief that follows dreaming. The same artificiality, Malfred knew, was evident in the printed book of fairy tales; it was clear that the illustrator had been thinking of Greece and Rome and not of AoteaRoa. Lettice Bradley, a gifted girl who, with Noni, could also draw the correct shadows of every object set before her, had made an unusual painting of Maui's fishing. She had lived and believed it. She "knew" the legend, with the Biblical force of the word "knew."

Malfred remembered that she had not given Lettice the praise she deserved for her painting; and she remembered why: she had been awed by it, had been envious of it and of the secret store from which Lettice had drawn her knowledge and understanding of times that she had never experienced. Other pupils could paint certain scenes with reasonable skill—Paris in the Spring, Hercules and the Twelve Labors, Jason and the Golden Fleece— of these, Malfred had never felt envious, for the store of knowledge was common, the track to it was worn, repaired, signposted, as tourist tracks are, with the usual red and white picnic tables— mushroom-shaped, with matching stools—along the wayside. How had Lettice Bradley—Malfred said the name to herself now, as she lay in the dark—how had Lettice Bradley found her way to the secret store? Noni, her rival in shadows and fire shovels had never found this imaginative abundance.

Lettice Bradley. Lettice Bradley, come out here and be punished. Lettice Bradley, stay after school. . . . Lettice Bradley who could never recite the terms of the Congress of Vienna or describe the Midland Railway network, or the importance of the Cheshire Salt Field or name the products of Birmingham—where had she visited in her dreams that she had been apprehended by the soul of her own country, like a calf branded early by the herdsman in whose paddocks it is born and by whose command it dies? Malfred had never been able to reconcile herself to Lettice

Bradley's gift that showed itself in this special way only. Oh, it hadn't been fair, it still wasn't fair that an ordinary schoolgirl whose acknowledged favorite reading was Rudyard Kipling and Zane Grey had been able to absorb, as a mindless sponge absorbs food from the sea, the myths and legends of her own country; and yet to live, as an ordinary schoolgirl with her ordinary family in a rough-cast, flat-roofed bungalow that had a vegetable garden with tall, tied beans at the back and a square of lawn in front, to be mown on Saturday afternoons or Sunday mornings!

No, it wasn't fair, Malfred said to herself now. In the years since Lettice Bradley blossomed in her painting of Maui, Malfred had seen the envy that she had known, seem to become part of the national character. All up and down the country people began to beat their fists on walls, doors, mountains, on the boles of trees in the bush, even on the clouds and the moon and the stars in their (suddenly) "own" sky, wanting to be let into the secret store, for the existence of it was no longer a secret. Someone, somewhere, had heard the rumor; the news was out; and it may have come to them, Malfred supposed—wiser now—from a source apparently more outlandish than Kipling and Zane Grey. It could have reached them through the Arabian Nights, or the Bible, or Shakespeare; or the current group of pop singers; or simply while they were staring at the garden spades and lawn fertilizer in the window of Woolworths. The news could have come through the waters of the Waitaki, it could have blown in the nor'wester—no one would ever know the source. But the news and the rumor of it had spread; it was part of daily life now to walk in the streets, stare at the people, and see the rumor in their eyes. The newspapers were full of it, and the beaches, the shops, the sports grounds; it was beaten out in the high, white boots of the marching girls; it was chanted in the pipes; it was boiled in the billy; and it rose from the lake with the seven-pound rainbow trout. It had flowed into the literature, the paintings; the country itself could not contain it; spontaneously, like a thistledown seed being carried by the wind as soon as it is ripe, it had spread "overseas" where, instead of the formerly academic "rumor" that, as official export had been subjected to such a lengthy quarantine that it had been forgotten or had died of the disease caught while it was being protected against the one it was feared to be suffering, it was now believed, it engendered new rumors that caused people to ask, turning their eyes to the Southern Hemisphere—Have you heard? Have you heard? They say . . . they say . . . Though such public asking does not often lead to the secret store, it may uncover new unsuspected treasures.

So one by one the items of national character became the center of the rumor and of the new probe to get at the treasure. Putting kowhai, puarangi, manuka, rata, tarapunga on postage stamps and biscuit tins (the first stage was insertion in poetry), selling Maori carvings, faked or genuine, in Lower Queen Street where the overseas ships berth—all helped, or was thought to help; at least it took advantage of the knowledge that the rumor was about and that people were heeding it. And Malfred knew or sensed, smiling in sympathy with those who were so desperate to stake a claim in the identity of their country, that so many people were now trying to falsify genealogical tables so that they might be able to trace an obscure relative who was a Maori! They could just as well and happily have found that their great-great-grandfather was a boiling mud-pool or a piece of glacier or a spray of kowhai or pohutukawa blossom! Malfred was re-

124

minded, by this national claim for identity, of the phase that children experience when discovering that they are separate beings; they disown their parents and dream themselves into the exciting newness, individuality, uncertainty, of having been "adopted." Malfred realized that her envy of Lettice Bradley had concealed an envy of all who had "known"—again in the Biblical sense: he *knew* her; she *knew* him—the myths and legends of the Maori, that is, an envy of the Maori who "knew" the land. For a time, then, she had felt ashamed that none of her great-grandfathers were native chiefs or her grandmothers Maori princesses. She thought of the Maoris as she thought of Lettice Bradley. It wasn't fair that they should know so much, instinctively, about their country; that, when they looked at the sky, they might think, without self-consciousness, of Rangi, while Malfred's image seemed a poor secondhand one of Gods reclining on clouds, eating lotus and hurling thunderbolts. She had grown out of this naïve approach to myths, for myths, like rivers, come out of the common sea and return there, and none is alone; an Identi-Kit dream of *Wanted National Identity* may have the face of Hercules and the body of Maui; it may be just plain Mum and Dad . . . nor does it matter whether one's blood has been mixed with lava or pohutukawa blossom. . . .

So I return to the pohutukawas, Malfred thought, these, and summer on Karemoana. And Wilfred . . . what was I thinking about Wilfred?

She gave a cry of surprise. She had been thinking that perhaps the prowler was Wilfred . . . returned from the dead. Her surprise was caused by her realizing that however hard he knocked at the door, and however long he stayed, she would never let him in.

· 17 ·

THEY HAD MET at the High School Jubilee, two years before the outbreak of the war, though their parents had known each other since their marriage, and Malfred, when she thought of a husband and children had said to herself, at times, wonderingly, "Who is the Anderson boy going with?" Their farm at Five Hills was one of the earliest established, most fertile, most profitable, and beautiful, in the province; and each of these attributes had its special glory. The Signal family had no "earliests" among their family. Malfred's grandparents had not arrived in the first ship, or set up the first farm or school or church, ploughed the first furrow, taught the first lesson, preached the first sermon. They had no claim to the first white child born in the North or the South Island, the first Prime Minister, member of Parliament, doctor, lawyer. . . . The staking of these claims mattered so much when there were no monuments to remind of illustrious ancestry, no gravestones to prove that even if forebears had no individual claim to glory, at least their names (hyphenated, sometimes tripled) could be traced back to the established, history-book heroes.

The Signal family had not even the reflected prestige of having attended the first lesson or the first sermon or the first session of Parliament. No one in the Signal family had "been there," or if they had, it had been in a role that was better forgotten or not talked about. Wilfred's family, on the other hand, had their quiver full of "firsts" and "earliests"—so full that the thought of them aimed itself at you every time you saw the Anderson brothers. They were assured boys, handsome, strong, with the appearance of "born" farmers, though David who was also killed in the war had already taken up Engineering in Christchurch. It was Wilfred who would have had the farm when his father died, who already managed it then as his father's health was failing. It was part of Wilfred's "dutiful" nature that he should attend the combined Jubilee Celebrations of the Boys' and Girls' High—his father had been among the first pupils, his grandmother had been the first headmistress of the Girls' High. Yet, he was a modest young man; he could afford to be; he had prized monuments to speak for him.

Malfred had been excited by the prospect of the School Jubilee. There had been a dreary, cold, wet winter. Malfred's mother and father had both been ill. Graham had been made a partner in the Law Office and it had seemed that everyone in Matuatangi was dying or making a will or suing neighbors, customers, relatives. Graham was restless, overworked; he kept saying it was time he "got out of" Matuatangi and went somewhere else—up north, perhaps, where he could get away from the "narrow provincialism" of Matuatangi. There was a chap at the office, he said, who got on his nerves—William Bertright, whom he remembered from the time when he used to go to the Law Office as a small boy when their father led the firm. William Bertright would be there, a smartly-dressed young man with a large face, small eyes, sharply-pointed nostrils like pen-nibs, with an intelligent, crafty look that relaxed into a pleasant smile when he faced the clients. He seemed always to be standing before huge, opened ledgers that were propped on a row of lecterns. There was a high stool but Graham never saw him sitting on it. Pen in hand William Bertright stood bending over the ledgers, all day, every day, writing in small neat figures.

When Graham first saw him, Bertright appeared young, eager, a bright youth among the old graybeards with the foreign names that were partners in the firm. Then Graham stopped going to the office. His father left the firm to teach, though he remained a partner. Graham did not see or hear of Bertright again until the day he walked up the wide steps to the Upper Chamber of the old Town Hall where the well-known, esteemed Law and Estate firms practiced beneath the gaze of the photographs of those honored in Matuatangi—the Mayors and the illustrious dead of the First World War. Graham swung the opaque glass doors open into the anteroom with its old-fashioned, waiting-room forms. The glass windows that separated the firm from the public were shut. Graham glanced through them, seeing the place as a member of the public might see it. What a clutter of papers, books, ledgers! The same old lecterns with new rows of bright, young clerks poring over them! Looking closer, Graham saw that the clerk at the end of the row appeared to be not so young; he was an old, white-haired man; his large face was creased with age; he scratched away with his sharp pen-nib while his nostrils were still pointed in their corresponding sharpness, as if his concentration were gathered there before it fell, like a dewdrop from a cold nose, on to the ledger.

"William Bertright. Good God, William Bertright!" Graham said. The writing on the wall—in the ledger—did it matter where the writing was? You couldn't forget it once you had seen it.

So at the end of winter Graham had taken the bold step of going north to Christchurch where a University mate (with an attractive sister) had set up a Law practice. Malfred missed Graham when he had gone north. Her father and mother were slow in recovering from their illness. It was only flu, yet it made them both depressed and irritable. Malfred had never realized before how much she had relied on her parents to set the mood of the day. She was the kind of person, then, who could not initiate her own moods, who remained most of the time on a level of placidity that, though she found it boring, she did not know how to change.

And to make everything worse that winter, Lucy had become a giggling schoolgirl, as collapsed as a paper bag and as unresponsive. Malfred thought, not wanting to remember her own girlhood, and weary of her Art classes where no one knew or was willing to know about the perspective and shading, "Oh, they should wrap schoolgirls in blankets, or shrouds, sew them, and hang them in trees, like chrysalids, until they are past the giggling stage!"

Then, with the spring, came revived interest in the School Jubilee. Malfred undertook to sit on the Folk Dance Committee, the Staff Social Committee, and to help prepare the Roll Call.

The night of the Staff Ball, Malfred had gone to help supervise the sixth form in preparing the supper. She had dressed with that extra care that distinguishes dressing for preservation and survival from dressing for conquest. She had hoped to dance, but no one had asked her, and she was "sitting out" with Miss Float, only half-listening to her traveler's tales. She was gazing dreamily at the couples, criticizing the band (imported from fifty miles up north when there were bands with as good a reputation in Matuatangi!), recognizing here and there the well-known citizens of the town and the country, noting who were Old Girls and who were Old Boys and wishing that the species didn't have such a definite air by which they could be known, yet feeling at home, too, cosy, proud, wanting nothing except perhaps to be asked to dance, interested in the Jubilee, its finale, its Roll Call, its success.

Then as she sat there it seemed suddenly that time, which had been running so smoothly to its destination, passing in a journey of triumph the scenery of the Jubilee and the past two crowded terms, went in a flash off the rails, overturned, changed the view. In only a few moments it had righted itself (temporal operators and operations were so expert these days) yet, to Malfred, the view seemed changed, the scenery inadequate, almost repelling, and there was Miss Float still sitting beside her prattling of Tudor Castles! All the Old Girls and Old Boys jigging around, all those white flowers at the back of the hall and on the stage, the white dresses of the girls in the upper forms—why was there so much *white*? It looked insipid, false, blurred. The color scheme was all wrong. Malfred felt the color burning inside her as she said, "It should be *crimson!*"

Yet she had helped to plan it; she had had no misgivings about it then. Old Girls, Old Boys. Roll Call. Tennis Teas. Mayoral Reception. And—worst—the permanent record, the magazine with its lists and lists of names (née so-and-so, née so-and-so), with prominence given to Old Girls who had lived overseas, as if they had achieved something by going overseas.

Malfred tasted a sick taste in her mouth. She closed her eyes. She saw, in place of the mass of white, the warm polished black of fire shovels filled with glowing embers. Then she opened her eyes and Wilfred Anderson was there asking her to dance, and the relationship that she had known in far-off school holidays at the farm when Wilfred's uncle and Malfred's father went climbing together in the Alps, was taken up again, easily, politely, with an undercurrent of excitement that neither mentioned at first but which both were aware of. Thought of the Jubilee faded from Malfred's mind. Traitorously, she did not go to the school sports. (Oh those fat girls in sacks, boards on heads, leaping into sand-pits! Oh the sheep-dirt where stray sheep had wandered onto the sports ground from the paddock next door!)

Malfred spent Sports Afternoon out at Wilfred's farm with Wilfred showing her the shearers' cottage, the slaughterhouse, the wool shed with its dark stink of grease and skin, animal and human; the horses, the dogs; then the house, big and old, with high ceilings and a bathroom the size of a barn; a house of kauri!

It was not the house that pleased Malfred most, though she wished it had been, with her approval acting as a signature to her domesticity. It was the paddocks and the fences that fascinated her; and the sheep, taking time off to stare, munching and staring, munching and staring, with their slotted eyes like black buttonholes in their white coats. It would be interesting to be a sheep farmer's wife, she thought, knowing that she could safely think this with some prospect of its coming true. (Unlike some women in their twenties, Malfred was not given to thinking dangerous thoughts or putting herself, in imagination, in daring but impossible situations. She dreamed as she shaded—keeping strictly to the outline of the object in view.)

She knew that Wilfred's family and the Signal family "approved" one of the other, that her mother would feel happier if she married Wilfred and made her home at Five Hills than if she married a Timaru or Christchurch man, or even someone from further down south. She was not so sure of her own feelings. In the months that followed she and Wilfred carried on a teasing friendship where both surveyed the darker undercurrent with pleasure and fear but made no move to plunge into it. They took part, instead, in practical affairs. They went to the Little Theatre Society plays, the Art Exhibitions; or they spent evenings at Five Hills and at the Signals' home where they talked, listened to the wireless, played lexicon. Then there were several months when they saw nothing of each other; and then, out of the blue, there was a weekend at the Hermitage that Malfred always preferred to think of as a "wicked weekend" when it was not so.

It was Miss Cotter, the Gym mistress, who encouraged her to stray from her usual staid fantasies.

"Go away for the weekend?" she said casually at Monday morning tea.

"Wilfred and I went to the Hermitage," Malfred said innocently.

"Oh! A wicked weekend!"

"Of course not!"

"Ah! A wicked weekend!"

Malfred relaxed. She enjoyed the sudden status she had acquired with the older and the younger teachers; she enjoyed it and at times deplored it; then she wanted to forget Wilfred, to return to her quiet life in the Art Room, the unobtrusive morning and afternoon teas in the staffroom when she talked earnestly about the problems of teaching Art and spent an enjoyably exciting few minutes switching Playground Duty with Miss Wallace or Library Duty with Miss Clode.

"Monday it is then!"

Triumphantly.

"Tuesday then! Done!"

Miss Clode's older face would be blotched pink with this unexpected excitement of staffroom tactics while Malfred would feel an exhilaration that she knew was out of proportion to the event. Still, what could one do? One had to have some pleasure, entertainment. On this basis the Jubilee, understandably, came as an event of wonder, approached almost in a state of delirium.

Miss Cotter repeated her insinuations. "A wicked weekend!"

Miss Cotter was just fresh from Training College and had introduced the new kind of Physical Training to the school. The old fashioned term, "Drill," was abolished, and the pupils and staff talked instead of Phys. Ed. Miss Cotter had introduced a new gym uniform, too—rompers—and she spent much of the time teaching dancing, Old English Country Dancing as well as Maori Hakas and stick games, with the girls changing from shepherdess costumes (white dresses, white sashes, coronets of flowers) for

Haste Haste Shepherds and neighbours
Shadows are falling, music is calling,
Come now leaving your labours,
Dance on the green till the close of the day.
Fair maids smile at our meeting,
Hands clasp hands in a greeting,
Hearts are joyously beating
In tune to the music of May . . .
Then come come come
Come shepherds all,
Trip so lightly dance so sprightly
Up the meadow and back again . . .
Now to crown the Queen of May
Deck her in garlands gay
Then lead forth in the ring
The gallant lad crowned as our King. . . .

All this on the dark varnished floor of the gymnasium, while outside, on the first day of May, the trees stood bare, their last few leaves blocked the drains, globules of ice lay in the hearts of the cabbages and on the frog ponds, and the sky was gray.

When they had finished dancing, in all their innocence, the fertility rites of another age and land, the girls became Maori maidens playing their stick games, singing the Maori words with the same kind of stoical bewilderment they had shown when, as Shepherdesses, they danced on the village green. They had performed as Shepherdesses at the Jubilee. They had danced at the motor camp near the Town Gardens, and had been a great success. While paradise ducks quacked in the Gardens' ponds, and women of the Croquet Club tapped away with their mallets, and the caretaker of the tennis courts plied the roller on the lawns in readiness for the coming season, the High School girls played Shepherdesses and Maori maidens and succeeded, Malfred thought, in being neither. She knew, too, that Miss Cotter, when her day's work was over, was herself interested in playing a more modern role that included "wicked weekends." Laura Cotter. Fresh-complexioned, fair, attractive. She had cast an eye at Wilfred on the night of the Staff Ball. Malfred was satisfied to feel that her own quieter "brown" type had claimed his interest. She knew that her face had a placid expression, that her brown hair, brushed three hundred strokes at bedtime, had a burnished shine in the plaits that framed her face. Her dress was muted, autumnal, tasteful, the color of woods and leaves; it did not trouble her that they were last year's leaves lying in decayed woods. She thought of birch trees, silver birch and beech and poplar; her father's interest in the evergreen native bush seemed strange to her then.

After the weekend at the Hermitage, with the rumors of war, the movement west of the Nazis, the speeches by the Prime Minister that where Britain went New Zealand would follow, Malfred's relationship with Wilfred became closer. Her home was near the Gardens. She and Wilfred walked in the Gardens, for they seemed, in a way, to be the gardens of her own home: so many of the spouting boys and lions, the drinking fountains, the exotic trees bore a plaque with her father's name on it; and the seats beneath the shady trees were dedicated to him.

Day after day they had walked together on the dry, dusty plains at the back of Matuatangi, on the straight, dusty roads with the gum nuts and gum leaves under their feet, knobbling the soles of their shoes; with the choking nor'wester dry in their throats. They had walked on the farm, through tussock, snow, grass, on the mounds of old rabbit warrens where the grass was rubbed from the earth and the countryside lay brown and gold, its skin exposed, like an old lion with the mange, with the wind scratching at its haunches and the bits of diseased fur being scattered about in the hills and valleys, while the lion lay tired, opening, closing, its amber, dust-filled eyes. Yes, they had walked, had skied, had ridden on horseback over the farm, and in the streets of Matuatangi and on the beaches, but it was in the Matuatangi Gardens that they spent their happiest hours, and it was here that they both chose to stare with pleasure and fear and anticipation into the darker undercurrent of their friendship. How false and formal they had been with each other, until then!

The fernhouse of the Gardens had been built many years ago, and stood to the left of one of the two main gates, in the deep shade of a row of umbrella trees. Though the walls and roof were of glass, they had long ceased to look like glass, for the atmosphere within exuded a green and yellow damp slime that clung to the walls and the ceiling, clouding the glass, making the darkened daylight within seem more dark and mysterious. The fernhouse was like a miniature artificial bush. Ferns overhung or sprouted in tubs; a noise of gushing creeks came from the one hose that sprouted water onto the ferns and shrubs and into a moss-lined pond. Never had there seemed to be so much water to spare; as if the genuine bush, learning of this artificial corner of itself in the Matuatangi Gardens, had sent part of itself there to strengthen the illusion of real bush. Unlike the human body that rejects an alien likeness, the bush, with ambassadorial welcoming had adopted, had grafted the fernhouse to itself.

Walking on the grass in the Gardens, Malfred and Wilfred had felt the dampness on their shoes and their feet. The grass was softly springing with rain, like moss. Yet, inside the fernhouse where there had been no rain, they found that their feet and legs were instantly soaking, and as they walked past the rows of ferns that drooped as if from a recent downpour, the fronds brushed a saturation of drops onto their coats and faces and hair.

It had been raining when they walked there for the last time together. Once inside the fernhouse they found again this phenomenon of an oozing, moss-lined, mysteriously rain-fed world. Malfred, turning to Wilfred, saw him in this dim, green bush-darkness. He saw reflected in her hair the green plait of pond slime that trailed across the ceiling of the house and down the walls onto the cold concrete floor. Smelling the moss was like breathing in soft, fine rain that had lain in the earth, had evaporated, then had fallen, exuding its own memorial, into their throats. Malfred shivered. The creeks, flowing from nowhere, trickled, gushed, bubbled. Some of the ferns were yellowing at the edges, dying in spite of the excess of moisture.

"Let's go out of here," Malfred said. Her voice was breathless.

Wilfred spoke slowly, stolidly almost. "Why?"

"Well, it's cold and damp. The sun never comes here. I don't know why *we* came here; with so much to do, and plan, and there's the Art Society Dinner, and this whole side of the Gardens is in shade all day. Look at that cracked window!"

Wilfred did not say, "To hell with the Art Society Dinner."

He took Malfred in his arms and kissed her, and she stood, surprised, warm, not knowing what to do.

"Give me your tongue," he said.

She felt alarm, then warmth again, and a taste of moss, like the green tongues of moss curled on the windows and the ceiling. And then, when Wilfred put his hand inside her dress she felt a damp steam, like sweating fern, rise from between her breasts. And then she jerked her head back and began to cry, and it seemed that all her gentleness flowed away with her tears, for she felt callous, aged, experienced, and she did not care when Wilfred, a deep flush spreading under his skin, said, "Excuse me," and went behind the wet, black-barked treefern, and she thought as they linked arms, easily now, and walked out of the fernhouse that the white specks and spatters on the fern looked like a new kind of mildew, a disease that the ferns had caught through being there, in the fernhouse, at that moment.

A month later Wilfred sailed with the troops, and she never saw him again. Nor did she ever go again to the fernhouse, though before she left Matuatangi forever she walked one afternoon through the Gardens and spent a half hour sitting in the sun on the stone seat of the Chinese Gardens that had been planted a year ago, with much ceremony, with dancing in the streets (dancing in the streets in Matuatangi!) and a Chinese feast put on by the Chinese community. The new Gardens replaced the old fernhouse which had been pulled down. These were dry, brilliant, formal gardens with miniature trees, a gold fish pond, an arranged stream (not creek) flowing decorously from a visible concrete channel. There were no ferns, no moss, and no shade, for the row of umbrella trees had been cut down. The fernhouse was gone forever.

This night of rain and wind had reminded Malfred of the fernhouse. She knew again, as she had known then, that if Wilfred had been outside knocking to get in she would not have let him in. She listened. She was pleased, now, to know that whoever knocked had not gone away. She heard again the footsteps swishing in the grass.

She said to herself, calmly, "The dark and the storm and the sea and the knocking may go on forever."

·18·

THE THOUGHT THAT THERE were no mountains on Karemoana gave Malfred a feeling of desolation. Lying in bed she looked suddenly from left to right to try to glimpse the snow, the familiar bulwark, chain, march of blue-white light that followed the country from north to south and gave (she thought) the South Islanders their exclusive strength as if their skeletons were rock and bone layered with snow. She was sure, as southerners are, of superiority, of a constitution that withstands cold, of the softer finer complexion of those whose faces are brushed season after season with soft fine misty rains. And once again, thinking of summer in the north, she felt afraid, as if at her age she had taken upon herself too great a challenge. Unknown people were

140

never as terrifying as unknown seasons and landscapes. A world where the earth was composed of nondescript mounds and folds, of extinct volcanoes (the people of Auckland had said to her, with pride, that their city was built on these craters), where summer nights, she had heard, meant sleeping almost naked, windows thrown open yet screened against mosquitoes, the air so humid that it was an effort to breathe, would never present the cool certainty of the south where, apart from an occasional slight earthquake, all was predictable, with the right weather in the right season, daffodils in spring, roses in summer, leaves turning gold in autumn, frost nipping the fingers and toes in winter. Oh, the seasons knew their place in the south, just as the Southern Alps knew their place in the dignity of the nation! Already Malfred was beginning to feel that the background of her life was being shredded, dissolved, that her coming north had seen an end to the fair play she had always known from the seasons, not as a discrimination because she was Malfred Signal, more involved in the landscape of her country than with its people, but as the right and expectation of a South Islander. And the fact that there were no mountains meant that there was no solid landmark in the background to refer to when the points of one's personal compass became confused. One's life could not suddenly flow and dissolve. The lights might go out, there might be storms and knocking, and no help in view but mountains seen out of the corner of the eye, as a white fortress; or daffodils seen and known in spring, and yellowing leaves in autumn were certainties that gave meaning and consolation, though one may not realize this until one had arrived in a strange landscape; a spring season where the daffodils and the leaves were already withered; where nothing was known or stayed or could be predicted.

What strength do the people in the north use to survive? Malfred wondered.

Why does no one realize that I need help, that I'm afraid to go out into the dark and cry out the words, "Help! Help!" Are all the people on the island asleep? Why does no one come?

Perhaps, she thought, the Constable had not been the most suitable person to call on the phone. Should she have called a minister of religion, a priest? She knew that the priest lived in a house overlooking the Kare bay, a popular resort in summer but now deserted except for the waves that peopled the sand with sighs, shells, stranded channels and pools. Malfred had called at the house to ask the way. The priest answered the door. He was dressed in a sweater and slacks, his skin was flushed, his eyes were faintly bloodshot.

"I've just come from a hot shower," he said, with a strong Irish accent.

Not knowing what to reply Malfred had hidden her confusion by remarking on the hot shower. "Oh!" she said. "You have hot water laid on!"

He was a priest, he was privileged in the lowliest matters of plumbing to the highest matters of belief. Everything must surely be ideal for him here on this island in this big old-fashioned, solidly-built house overlooking the bay. Malfred noticed that the church itself had a shabby holiday appearance; a prefabricated afterthought. The churches of three denominations were almost side by side in the same road, with the Presbyterian Church set behind the manse of which the front door opened almost to the road with a few feet of rock garden between the door and the road. The minister's study could be seen through the window. Bookshelves, desk with his telephone, the elderly minister sitting at his desk poring over church papers—almost as if to say, "Here I am, the Presbyterian minister busy with church affairs. I have my study here so that you can see me as you pass, and realize that I work during the week, not only on Sunday, that much preparation goes to make up my sermons. You can walk in the city, up and down Queen Street, looking in the shop windows where, for your entertainment and instruction, you can see washing whirling inside washing machines, cosmetic displays, motor mowers mowing, painters painting, builders building. Only here, in Karemoana can you see a minister engaged in preparation for ministering."

The priest rubbed a large, warm, red hand under his chin. He's not even had time to dry himself, Malfred thought. Then he held out the same steamed hand to introduce himself.
"Father Cawston."
Malfred was disconcerted.
"Oh!"
He seemed to be more of an athlete than a priest. Malfred explained that she had bought the white house on the hill—yes, the one where the elderly woman had lived, the white house with the view, and could he kindly tell her in which direction was Followdale? "Where you catch the planes."
"You're catching the plane?"
"Oh no, I just wanted to get my bearings."
Father Cawston smiled in a secretive yet friendly way, as if to say, "We must allow people their eccentricities, their dependence on objects, landmarks, what you will, to get their bearings. This newcomer to the island finds it necessary to walk three miles out of her way to discover where she is and what she must do in

an emergency. One who is at home with the true church has no need to waste time and energy in such pursuits. God provides the bearings, the places to turn to in times of emergency."

He smiled again, but his smile was in no way superior. He directed Malfred to the airport and Malfred set out down the long, dusty road to the flat tidal area where the twin-engined amphibian came in to land. Here were the slums of the island. Sparse vegetation. Decayed houses. A tidal bay with its black sands littered with sea scum, papers, packets. Malfred noted where the plane landed and where it would be necessary for her to get her ticket. The office was next door to the carriers who, in true island democracy and impartiality, delivered firewood, removed furniture, carried all goods small and large, including coffins empty or filled; the carriers were also the undertakers of the island.

The more Malfred thought of phoning the priest, the more she found it hard to resist the impulse. After all, she thought, the prowler may be a churchgoing person. My phoning Father Cawston may bring the prowler to his senses. He may leave me in peace at last. I shan't sleep though. Surely morning will come soon? I know with the experience of my fifty-three years that morning always comes; light has filled the sky every morning of my life. What need have I to depend on stupid prowlers to switch on my meager ration of electricity when morning will come soon to provide all the light I need to see?

Once again Malfred crept out of bed and made her way to the sitting room to the dead telephone on its shelf beside the Karemoana maps, the pile of old *Reader's Digests* and *Argosies* that had not belonged, Malfred was sure, to the former owner of the house but to long-gone mythical or real holidaymakers who spent a wet, stormy Labor Weekend gazing out over the gulf and its islands while they flipped the pages of, *Have You Got Cancer: A Sure Way to Tell; My Most Wonderful Human Experience; Life Is What You Make It; Have You Signed Your Own Death Sentence?*

Malfred thumbed through the pages of the old telephone directory, Karemoana West, found the presbytery number, lifted the receiver, heard the muffle of nothing, dialed the number, waited a few moments, then began to speak.

"Is that you Father Cawston? You may not remember me. I've just bought the white house on the hill. Yes, I moved in there recently. I asked you to direct me to the airport—oh, you do remember me?"

She was pleased that he remembered.

"Father Cawston, I wonder if you may be able to help me? I'm already in touch with the police who are expected any minute, but I think that perhaps this may be in your province—yes, I know that the members of various professions have provinces and must keep to them; they mustn't trespass!"

Oh why, Malfred wondered, do I have to speak in this stilted manner?

"Father Cawston, a prowler who is possibly a member of your church has been at my door since half past nine this evening, knocking, knocking, knocking, and when I refused to open the door he (she spoke the sex of the prowler with certainty now) had the effrontery to switch off my lights at the meter box outside. Do you think you could come to the house to persuade him to leave me alone? Yes, it may be something that you can deal with more readily than the Constable. Oh no, I've no idea who it may be. As you know, I've only recently come to live on the island and I've not yet had a chance to get to know people—only the tradespeople, so far—the restaurant proprietor, the woman in the shop at the corner, the Road Board employee sitting high and dry inside the cab of his yellow grader—why are graders and bulldozers painted that hideous yellow?—the man driving the refueling lorry; the neighbors, an elderly man and woman who are building an extra room to their house; I've not even had a chance to get to know the vegetation, though I've tasted the oranges—they're bitter."

Her voice went like a shriek into the telephone, she did not know why, when she described the taste of the oranges. Why should they have been bitter?

"Oh yes, I understand. Yes, I expect to make one or two friends while I'm here, not many, for my aim in coming here is to study the landscape itself, the vegetation, the earth, the sea, and if I feel so moved, to paint it as I see it. I have my paints all ready, all laid out, and I've done preliminary sketches of my New View but the moment hasn't come to put my new seeing to paper; at the moment I'm concerned with my safety, my life. Yes, I shall paint the earth uncluttered by human beings. Oh? I'm not a religious person but it is possible that He did make a mistake. The Garden of Eden would still be a pleasant place if they hadn't taken the command so seriously. No, I've not been turned away from Paradise, I'm not indulging in spinsterly backbiting. Club for the lonely? How dare you! How dare you, you with your hot water laid on! If I were not so mature and stable I should hang up this minute. I'm an educated woman. I've spent years of my life teaching children to draw objects; still life was my passion, though I never thought, until now, of the incompatibility of the two words. How can *Life* be *still?* Or how can anything which is *still* be *alive*—in the eyes of schoolgirls, I mean, and Art teachers who cannot see deep into the restless center of a tone?

"Yes, I am grateful that you do understand my intention in coming here to spend my retirement. Oh? I look forward to seeing them, I have heard that in a good year when they are in bloom along the coast the island has the appearance of being ringed with fire. Hell is *your* comparison. Both sea and fire may be necessary barriers, protection for the derelict souls. No, I have not known them before; it is all new—the deceitful seasons, the warm wind blowing from nowhere, the islands near and sharply-defined in rain. And the mangrove swamps, how can you explain them, each tree separate, standing with its head just above water. A sermon? Yes, knocking, knocking all evening. Something has delayed the police. You are tired, you have a long day ahead tomorrow, you must attend a consecration in the city?

"Father Cawston, are you there? I knew when I rang you that it was entirely out of your province. Forgive me for having supposed that the human heart has no boundaries."

Malfred replaced the receiver, wiped the dust from her fingers, turned, idly, the pages of a rain-faded *Reader's Digest.* The windows cannot be stormproof, she thought; no window could be, against this driving wind and rain from the sea.

Life's Little Humorous Episodes. It Pays to Increase Your Word-Power. The Man Who Rose from a Shilling-a-Week Errand Boy To Become the Millionaire-Owner of International Chain Stores! How You Too Can Learn the Secrets of Finance. Has That Sore on Your Lip Healed? The Heart-Rending Story of a Woman Who Waited Too Long. A Moving Human Condensed Book: I Was Made An Honorary Chief in a Tribe of

Headhunters. Over One Million Copies Sold! Condensed for quick easy reading; acclaimed by the busy financier and professional man, the readers who snatch time from a heavy schedule to *keep abreast,* in train, bus, plane, between TV programs, with the *cream* of international literature specially chosen by our world-roaming literature scouts. . . . (Though how, Malfred wondered, does one *keep abreast* of the *cream* of something unless one is a midnight mouse trapped in a jug of milk?)

She read the first sentence of the "moving human story" . . . "Towards the close of World War Two a small insignificant man stood, one day in spring . . ."

She realized the trend, the comfort of it all; no one would have dreamed it of him; besides, insignificance can be most painfully felt in *spring.*

Then, once again, she picked up the receiver, listened, dialed a number, and waited for the pitch of nothing to reach her ear. He will be in bed, she thought. They discourage night calls. If people are so intent upon keeping to their province perhaps he will find that this affair does lie within his province. The prowler could be ill. How do I know that he is not bleeding slowly to death, and his impulse to keep knocking at my door is born of his having recognized in me someone who may be able to rescue him? Perhaps he needs help? Yet, it is so strange; it is only those legendary "old soldiers home from the wars" who knock at doors in the middle of the night when a storm rages outside; and then, in the story, the door is opened to them, they are made welcome, given a bowl of hot soup ("steaming" is the word used), they are stripped of their ragged blood-stiffened uniforms, their wounds are bathed and bound, they are put to bed between fragrant sheets, with their head resting on feather pillows. . . . And the owner of the cottage, going downstairs to attend the fire and bolt the door for the night, knows the tenderness and the pride of possession as she touches the stained uniform and moves the tall, mud-caked boots out of direct range of the fire's flames.

It was ever thus, Malfred thought, changing in her mind to archaic expression, with "old soldiers home from the wars." It was ever thus, and never as it has been, with the soldiers not old but young, and not going at once to bed but drinking whisky to drown their memories, and then weeping because the whisky made them remember, and then stamping on their experience, giving a hearty good-natured shout, catching the early bus to town to fill in the form for the Rehabilitation Grant.

Yet the prowler outside may be an enemy, someone whom, in the past, I've hated or who has hated me. Someone, perhaps, whom I've envied. Yet I've not indulged in envy—indulgence needs time and devotion. I've been stabbed by it, I've felt pain and hate many times but my nature is my own surgeon and has removed my discomfort almost immediately, discarded it, left within the wound, perhaps a tiny tip of ill will that I've not noticed again, or that has given pain that I've not been able to locate, having forgotten the original wound. . . .

"Oh, is that you, doctor? Yes, this is an emergency. I've not met you, I've no intention of meeting you professionally. Yes, I'm new."

She looked down at herself and smiled at the irony of her description.

"I've moved into the white house on the hill, with the flax bushes in front, overlooking the gulf and its islands. No, I am no relation to the former owner. Yes, some of her books are here, a little of her furniture, a few scattered possessions. She had no relatives? There's a small tin box of photographs, and another tin box with leatherbound volumes of the poets—Keats, *The Golden Treasury, Sonnets from the Portuguese.* The photographs are stained and brown as if the rain or the salt air, perhaps the sea, has corroded them. There's a man who must have been her father—a slightly built, shy-looking person, with the appearance of having a limp, and with his head set on one side. He's in mountaineering clothes, boots, windjacket, a framed rucksack on his back; strange gear for one who looks so slight and delicate in health. He's leaning on an ice axe. The words scrawled in pencil on the back of the photo read. 'Beyond the Southern Lakes.' The other photo is of a young man in soldier's uniform— the former owner's fiancé, I should think; perhaps her brother, but I hardly think so. He's a strong, attractive-looking young man, but there's something indefinably unpleasant about him, though it's really hard to see him so clearly, for the photo is specked with mildew.

"But you know the place, why should you want me to give you more details?

"Just outside the window of this room there's a half coconut shell hanging to entice the birds to feed here in winter. I know that bellbirds and tuis come, and the wax-eyes peck for the honey in the flax flower and fatten themselves, no doubt, on the plump figs. And there are subtropical flowers, a tree at the back door. I feel, when I talk of this subtropical world as if I'm being borne upstairs, upstairs near the sun; it seems so remote from down south. Yes, I'm afraid."

Malfred groaned suddenly.

"Oh no, I've no pain anywhere. I get breathless and tired, but one expects that at my age. Yes, I sleep well. No, no vomiting. Yes, an emergency. Since half past nine last evening (it must be long past midnight now) there's been someone knocking violently at my door; also they've been switching off my light from the meter box outside the front door. I think it may be someone who needs your help. No, though I've heard the knocking, and the swish in the grass outside, like footsteps. Yes, he may be unhinged; perhaps he's armed. No, I never dream—well, seldom. My nerves are as steel."

Malfred set her lips primly together, then repeated, "My nerves are as steel."

"Of course it's an inept description of nerves, but what kind of semantics do you expect in the middle of the night?

"Yes, I'm afraid. I'm being watched, stalked; someone is waiting to get into my house, and it may be a madman. You don't use that expression these days? Well, mentally unbalanced, then; it means the same thing and it takes more energy and room to say it but I suppose one must sacrifice personal economies to compassion. Pease come to try to reason with him, doctor. No, I've no drugs in the house. Aspirin, yes; nothing else. No, I've told you I've not actually *seen* anyone but there's someone outside knocking, prowling, waiting. I don't think I can bear the strain of it much longer. Please. I've phoned the police. They're coming as soon as they can. (She spoke in reassuring plural.) I've phoned Father Cawston, too. No, he thinks that perhaps it's in your province. I've a feeling that whoever is outside is in great distress and may act violently at any moment; there's a desperation in his knocking, and the choice of such a night, with storm, rain, wind, to prowl the island bears out my intuition: there will be *violence* before long, doctor. Plunging my house from light to darkness to light must give him a sense of power that may get out of control. No, the priest would say that it's different with God. I'm quite sure Father Cawston can explain the difference, if he believes there is one.

"You feel then, that this is a matter for the police? I had the idea that your profession had gone a long way towards helping these people rather than leaving them to be dealt with by the police. They need understanding. A medical man, quietly spoken, tactful, calm, could help. You recall the doctor who, the other day, talked to the man on the Empire State Building, persuaded him not to jump, but to see reason. Oh? You wonder if it *was* reason that he saw? You mean, you can't mean, that you think his problem would have been solved if he had jumped?"

Malfred spoke coldly now.

"It was only an illustration. Of course there's no Empire State Building on Karemoana—unless the sea has built its secret one. Karemoana is a derelict, dead island, the 'Skid Row' of the South Pacific. It has encroaching, self-confident mangroves; it has pohutukawa trees: fireworks in summer, rusting the earth when their sparkle and bloom are finished; it has white manuka; high, dusty roads that overlook the sea; wet valleys of bubbling creeks and treeferns and deserted shacks with drawn blinds; it has, too, its own corner of the South Island—swamp, flax, ridged hills that are best for photographing for calendars and overseas magazines, a stockman riding against a background of sky; and it has sheep, sheep with fine wool; it has huge, brilliant flowers growing not on stalks but as branches; it has outsize butterflies that are so heavy with color that their flight is a skimming stagger from flower to flower; it has smoky-gray moths, their wings edged with blue; lemon trees, banana palms, fig trees . . ."

Malfred paused, out of breath with speaking and with the wonder of Karemoana.

"I beg your pardon? Yes, I realize that you administer to people, that the sad, retired people have come to spend the rest of their days sitting in the brilliance and shade of jacaranda and frangipani. Yes, I know there's social life on the island, there's the island newspaper, there's the Cultural Association, the Community Association, the Road Board, the Labour Party Meetings, with free bus transport; the T.A.B., also with bus transport, not free; there's walking, swimming, fishing; there's the hydrofoil, knees-up, white-painted bride cutting a dash with the waves, filly-prancing to and from the city; there's the old ferry, warm, creaking, salt- and rain-spattered lower deck, a permanent pool of sea near the railings; the old ferry with its cups of tea, biscuits, pinky bars; the landing at downtown Queen Street where you can sit on a pigeon-messed seat and eat fish and chips or oysters and chips and think, What a fine city, none of its ugliness, past, present or to come, can destroy the beautiful fact that it lies with its downtown heart open to the sea.

"Yes, I'm becoming sentimental. I do come from the south. Originally. I don't know why, when I'm asked that question, I always add that mysterious word—originally. Yes, I know that when the sea wants its own way it always gets it, with peaceful coexistence or with violence or any other means. Yes, I realize that you may think I'm a depressed new settler making an emergency call in the middle of the night because I've no one else to talk to; you think you've solved my problem with this kindly chat about Karemoana. I'm sorry, doctor, but it's not that way at all. Naturally I'm interested in Karemoana. I'm aware it has people and other vegetation, and wild cats, too, that vanish with a witchlike scream into the manuka scrub; but my reason for waking you at such an hour is that there's a prowler who's been knocking at my door since past nine this evening, and I think it may be someone in need of your help. Do you think you could come as soon as possible? It may be a matter of life and death."

Malfred found that she savored the words as she said them. She remembered the court case, recently reported in the newspaper, of a woman who idolized a footballer, and tried to get to him, the hour before the big game, a special message of encouragement which she felt would help him, though he had never seen her face and never knew her name. She was in despair when the switchboard operator insisted that no communication could be put through unless it was a matter of life and death. What else could the poor girl do but invent a story of sudden death? At least the footballer received a message from her. And here she was now, in Wellington jail because magistrates and switchboard operators could not really distinguish when a matter became a matter of life and death, because there was no way of telling.

"Yes, it may be a matter of life and death."

Slowly Malfred repeated the words that came to her over the dead phone. Where had the phone picked up such quietness, on this night of wind and storm? Surely everything had its audible heartbeat on such a night? Everything, it seemed, but the disconnected telephone.

"Yes. You feel that in the circumstances the affair is a matter for the police, that it is outside your province. No, doctor, I have no need to make an appointment with you, there is no need for consultation about my own affairs. Thank you, doctor. Good night."

Malfred sighed and replaced the receiver. She flipped once again the pages of the *Reader's Digest*. *Do you want to Win a Round-the-World-Trip for Two?* How did one manage if one was alone and won the Round-the-World-Trip for Two? She supposed that the sponsors coped tactfully with that situation. *How I Learned To Be Noble,* by Peter Guild Junior. (The gossip columns of the world portrayed Peter Guild Senior as being ignoble.) *The Case for a Regular Medical Check-up. Your Lungs May Be Fooling You.*

Malfred went back to bed and lay with her eyes closed. She listened. All was silent. Wind, sea, rain seemed to have grown quiet. The knocking had ceased. She strained her ears, intent on the silence. She had the feeling that perhaps nothing mattered any more, that there were no other people living in the world, that even the small holiday baches scattered on the hill above the gulf were now deserted forever, with the springy grass, the gorse, the white manuka, golden ice plant growing up through their decayed floors, with black mould spotted on the faded cretonne curtains; with long processions of ants moving to and from last summer's honeydrops, sugar crystals, rim-blackened lidless tin of golden syrup; with the island, that had never smelt of people, even in the days of the moa hunters, that had the smell only of white manuka, moss, wild flowers, seeped now in formic acid, the racial smell used to preserve the dead of other worlds. Ants were insects new to Malfred's experience. Oh, there had been ants down south, a few observed in the Gardens, but down south the ants never presumed to take over an entire house. Here, up north, they seemed to know their power. Malfred had seen them stopping to gossip with each other, combing their plaits for news; or one, apart, would seem to be shouldering a stray crumb towards the dark winter tower; others drew swords to kill, then walked round and round the quad to pay for their crime. In the ant world news day seemed to be hairdressing day, with a shape of smell and touch being interpreted as a detailed map of the promised feast, the enemy, the excitement center, roads to home. It was possible that now all the deserted baches on the island lay preserved in the smell of ants, that for the taste of one drop of last year's honey this diplomatically small dragon-world had invaded, moved like an endless line of refugees who, hearing this rumor of sustaining sweetness, had come to hoard it through winter; but to the refugees the sweetness was love, the buds turning black under a wintry sky when no warm feelings bloomed, bore fruit or ripened.

So the ants had taken over, and the spiders lay once more at ease on the bottom of the old galvanized iron baths, and the slaters crept between the damp folds of last summer's newspapers; the wetas came inside, too; and the wasps, the moths, the mosquitoes, rats and mice; possums thudded on the roof; mynahs cackled and squawked at the front doors; kingfishers possessed with flame the dead telephone wires; fantails danced in the porches or fluttered in and out through the picketed doors of the brokendown dunnies.* It was an old fantasy, this re-possession of the land by the exiled plants, insects and animals. It was a convenient way, Malfred knew, of getting rid of the human race

* Wooden "outhouse."—*Ed.*

without committing genocide. And why not get rid of them if none came to help in the night, in the dark and the storm? If not even those who were "qualified," the official helpers, would answer the call?

Malfred knew that she was not brave enough to run from the house to fetch a neighbor—supposing there were neighbors left alive. She thought of the woman who had died in the house. What had happened to her? No one had told Malfred the cause of her death; perhaps it was old age. Did she die in the night? Was there a storm with the rain lashing the windows as if they were portholes of a sinking ship? Malfred felt that perhaps now there was no one to whom she was closer than to the former owner of the house. Why had the woman come to Karemoana to retire? What had she hoped to find here? Or what had she hoped to lose? Sitting at her front door watching the fantails in the flax flowers and the kingfishers on the wires; staring out at the gulf and its islands; reading the *Sonnets from the Portuguese,* Sonnets of John Keats, "The poetry of earth is ceasing never; on a lone winter evening, when the frost has wrought a silence"; or "When I have fears that I might cease to be . . ."; or reading the little book of Omar Khayyám; or the program for the Coronation Service in Westminster Abbey. There had not been time to discuss the owner with the neighbors although Malfred had heard the woman in the grocer's talking about her, how she had helped to bathe Miss Corlett.

"There's nothing much you can hide when you're naked," the woman in the grocer's had said.

Malfred did not agree but to keep the peace she had murmured, "No, there isn't."

"And she and I used to sit in the sun looking at the birds in the flax flowers. When the flax flowers are out I suppose you will be sitting in that basket chair looking at the flax flowers?"

How desperately this woman wanted things to remain unchanged! I shall be painting, Malfred thought, but did not say. Just one or two pictures to get down my view of the world now that it is uncluttered by people. I shan't be sitting, disease-ridden, in a basket chair at my front door waiting for the end.

Had there been a prowler before, in Miss Corlett's day? Malfred wondered again. He may have forced entry once, but it was impossible for him to get in tonight. All windows were fastened. The doors were locked and bolted. Malfred closed her eyes, sighing, as the same thoughts came again and again into her mind. The windows, the doors, would the knocking start again? Who was it? When would help come? With her eyes closed she looked as helpless as she felt; she looked a tired woman of fifty-three, weary with years of service and of human selfishness, of trying to solve problems unaided, or turning to rivers and seas and mountains when human beings, unaware of her need, failed her; and now she sat sighing, exhausted from a night-long struggle to try to keep out a desperate, possibly violent intruder.

She breathed slowly, deeply. There was an ache in her breast. She could not quite locate it or explain it until she realized that the silence had remained, that it had fallen like an irremovable weight upon her body, the room, the house, the island, the world. It was not merely a gap in the sound through which one could peer into the stillness; it was utter silence spread like a sealing blanket, from world's edge to world's edge, from night to night.

It's no use any more, Malfred thought. Even if the police, the doctor, the priest were to try to rescue me they could not penetrate the silence. It is too late now and too dark and I am too old. What use is it for me to try to mine light and color from such darkness?

·19·

IT WAS NOT A muffled or depressed sound. Acoustic tiles did not line the sky, the earth and the sea to keep out the roar of wrath and pride, the noise of growing, of being; it was true silence. It was not the tired silence that followed and was part of a storm. It was new, first silence, emerging from emptiness, from nothingness. It was not the tolerance of silence that exists side by side with scrapings of sound, whispers, rustling, shuffling, murmuring. It was tyrannical silence, a dominion of silence over all sound. Death, Malfred supposed, and had thought she knew, was silence; but death was the silence of absence, of the empty house where the tenants have gone, of the street where the children do not play any more. This could not be the silence of absence for it seemed to exist where nothing had ever been and thus had ever gone away; a tyrannical, cunning silence subject to change because it had the essence of knowing that all attributes and objects change; it simply could not be caught out in its perfection. It did not bring fear or pleasure or wonder; it brought itself.

Malfred did not now how long it lasted. She struggled to ally it to her past experience—to death, tiredness, soundlessness; but it was no use. Nor did the oblique approach to it work any more successfully. She could not stare through it, ignoring it until she reached the end or the other side, then exclaim in the uproar, "It is Sound! Silence is but a facet of sound." She had learned to beware of the telescopic, fashionable, so-called poetic thinking that calls the beginning the end and the end the beginning, that marries opposites in order to unite them and decrease the effort of trying to understand their separate natures. Surely there was never any such silence on earth or in the sky, and if there had been no one had been willing to recognize it.

Even in the television film that Malfred had seen, of the stars and the planets in space, there had been an accompaniment of "space" music because the thought of silence had been too terrifyingly unacceptable. And the myth of that haven of silence, the world beneath the sea, could not be dreamed of any more, for the recording machines played the singing, barking, sighing of fish, the tremuli of seaweed, the thunderous wave-echoes in caves and sea-bed ravines. There was an obsession of man to prove that everything uttered had language, patterns of sound; if it were not the fish singing, it was stars, mountains, trees making their cosmic "noise"; the universe was a place of everlasting noise. Nor was it possible to believe now that the room "two inches behind the eyes" contained the true silence, for dreams were born there, and it was being said now that the principal content of dreams was noise, that dreams were a noise in the mind and if they had meaning it was related not to memory or thought but to the patterns of sound made by the brain; that a new sound-alphabet was being constructed—the alphabet of dream-noise.

Everywhere the denial of silence, the insistence upon sound had made a confusion, a noise of living. But to experience this true silence, was it necessary to suffer a night of storm, wind, rain, knocking?

The silence could not last, Malfred knew. Already it was collapsing at its boundaries, settler noises were making their way into the lonely, fertile place where they could make their homes, breed their sounds. Soon there would be no square or drop or shadow of silence left. As she almost watched the silence vanishing, Malfred felt that there was some action she should have taken while she had been alone in the silence; there was something she ought to have done, she could not think what it might have been; something that should have been thought of or dreamed while the silence belonged to her. It was too late now. Outside, the released flax spears shook in the rising wind, the sea came again into being; Malfred could hear the distant comforting hush-sh-sh. She knew that at the back of the house the big fir tree had set itself moving and sighing once more while on the island road going down to the bay, the valley plantation of infant pines that oozed a green polish of light that the wind rubbed and streaked in the sky would have started again their faint sea-murmuring, Ah-Ah-Ah!

She heard the boards of the house creak, groan; a scatter of leaves on the roof; a scraping of mice or rats in the wardrobe. She turned on the light above her bed. A black beetle crept carefully, like a waiter balancing a round, shiny tray on his head, along the edge of the carpet. There was a sudden thud, first against the window pane, then in the room. Something had got in through the crack at the top of the window that Malfred had sealed with a strip of old pillowcase to keep out the rain. Thud-thud. A drunken knocking against the window, the wall, and now above Malfred's head, near the bedlight. A big moth with black-patterned wings and heavy body was knocking itself against the light; its lit eyes gleamed amber; as if starved, it surged again and again upon the light, drawing food to the gaunt poverty of the darkness that it had known and absorbed outside in the night.

"An old story," Malfred said impatiently. Seizing the *Listener*, she flapped it upon the wall, and the moth was killed, and Terror Fancy, the pop singer smiling in his life-sized photograph, fell from the middle pages of the *Listener*. A dusty fragment of moth-wing fell to the floor. Terror Fancy's face was wet with squashed body.

Malfred looked up at the window. One or two insects, a daddy longlegs and a few moths were prancing against the pane, fixing their eyes close to the scene, like paupers gazing in to a feast of light and warmth.

"Oh, the senselessness of it!" Malfred cried. "Keep out, can't you!"

Why was there so much need, this one evening of her life, for insects and people to invade her new home?

And the weather, too. It was raining again, the rain trickled down inside the window, splashed on the sill, the drops just missing the bedclothes. It wasn't like this a few hours ago, Malfred thought. Nothing came in then. My house was insectproof, waterproof. I was safe. Even the apparently senseless knocking could not gain the prowler entry to my home. It will be strange when morning comes, if morning ever comes again, and I go outside, unafraid, into the daylight, and see the flax bushes and the manuka, the fig tree, the lemon tree, the marigolds, and the ice plant, its golden fringes opening in the sun, and remember what this night has been, with its storm and fear and knocking and silence, and then, at the end of the silence, the insects that came in to feast and die, almost as if they were borne on the last wave of silence; the insects and the rain, and the wind that is in the room now, shaking my dress that is draped over the chair. These intruders are parasites of the silence.

She reminded herself then that she would have to report the prowler. She would telephone the Constable. He would call at the house, sit at the table in the sitting room, take out his notebook, and write down her words, but when he read them over to her, they would not be her words, they would be official words, belonging to nobody, and they would say, "I retired to bed at approximately nine p.m. At approximately nine fifteen, hearing a sound outside my window, I switched on the light, rose, whereupon . . ."

Oh, it would not be fair if her ordeal were translated thus. It would be false. Yet she would be asked to sign it, and she would not refuse, and she would say, "Will you have a cup of tea, Constable?" and be pleased when he said, "No thank you," and she would see him to the door, and his last words, after he admired the view from the front door over the gulf and the islands would be, "We'll catch them, never fear." But as he said goodbye he would look at her thoughtfully as if to say, "Women living on their own are often nervous, under strain, inclined to let their imagination run away with them. They're all alike, these retired schoolteachers, lonely, dreaming up a man, then getting terrified when their imagination takes over where their desire left off!"

Malfred was used to this judgment of her, and though it tended to make her conform to it in spite of herself, she was tolerant of those who saw her in this light; they were like miners who see things in the light cast by the lamp fixed to their own head: they made their own seeing, in their own light.

She settled once again to rest, to the luxury of thinking about morning, about the island and her life there. Her life would be orderly, in that way excluding outward eventfulness. She would get up at the same time every morning, go to bed at the same time each night. She would allot to each day its special household, gardening, shopping or artistic duty. She would forget Matuatangi, the south, the rivers, her dreary years as a teacher. She would arrange a studio in one corner of the large sitting room, near the window, in the full intense light of the sky and the sea that glittered and winked a million darting fish of light. Some of that light she knew, or hoped, would splash onto her paper or canvas. She would walk with a dream of it in her head, shuffling the spectrum over and over behind her eyes, as if dealing herself in the last, inevitably fatal, most absorbing game she had chosen to play, packs, queens, kings, knaves of light. The colors would range themselves side by side in a picketfence of light; then, desperately, she would tear down each paling, to see the darkness it enclosed and concealed. In the south she had not known such intensity of light, of the kind that at midday seems to sweat in its own dazzle, to bathe itself in a quivering mist that comes down over the sea and the islands and over the treefern and the manuka, clouding all to jungle green. She would paint it all, she told herself, as she saw it. She would paint the clay bank at the back of the house with its succulent, starred ice plant and the red flower that was opening from a leafless tree, like a tropical bird pinned between bare twigs, just outside the kitchen door. She would paint the marigolds, the flax bush, the thin, light brown stalks of grass that grew, light-space between each stalk softening them and clinging to them, like light-fur. Perhaps, after all, in a land where bulldozers were people, motor mowers were people, buses were people, where all things were people except, it seemed, the people themselves, she might be taking risks in trying to paint the islanders, for their teeth might be the fangs of bulldozers filled with clay, and their hair might be stiff, marigold petals, their faces gray mud-flats pimpled with weeds, their eyes mangrove pools. She did not know, she did not know yet how she would paint what lay around her, but this night, in the midst of the storm, the calm, the knocking that ceased and began and ceased, she set herself, to try to keep calm, as if it were an examination question she must answer, the preliminary dream, her seeing, her choosing, her setting it down in pictures, the earliest most vivid kind of writing that included the shadows of things seen, not separating object and shadow, not exposing the object to the striking down of the sun, but folding the shadow within the object itself.

The preliminary dream: she would walk on the island, she would talk to the inhabitants, in the channel of speech that middle-aged, retired schoolteachers most know, in common with derelict people and fly-by-nights and the shy and withdrawn;

exchanges with tradesmen, public servants, passers-by. The postman careering in his blue van along the road; the postman, always a great favorite, hated, longed for, feared, loved. Even on Malfred's first day in Karemoana, in her taxi ride from the ferry, the driver had pointed out the house where the postman lived.

"Postman lives here, in case you want to get in touch with him any time.

"He lives quite close to you," the driver added, as if uncertain that Malfred had realized her distinction and good fortune.

And Malfred had answered, trying to memorize the position of the house and yet trying to appear not to do so, "That's useful."

At the same time wondering what use was there. Heartbeats were no longer quickened by the sight of a man who brought only sample coupons for detergent in mustard-yellow folders, or discount offers for Encyclopedias of Art, stressing the thousands of "items" recorded. So much news of Art, written by experts. Malfred knew there would be a chapter on Proportion and Perspective; the street, the gate, the path leading up to the house, the hills beyond. Distance is blue. Snow is white. Sunsets are pink. The sun rises in the east and sets in the west.

Malfred had obeyed all the laws of seeing and of communicating to others what is seen; now, carefree, a criminal of vision, she came and went as she pleased, or she *would do so,* she *would,* when morning came and all was well. But had not other people dramatically changed their scene and share of sky and neighbors in skin, had set in motion a preliminary dream of which the one tragically constant feature was the way it stayed preliminary? How many sat now in the waiting room of might-have-beens, turning page after page of faded color plates depicting themselves caught fast in their preliminary dream?

Outside the storm continued, not as fierce as it had been. The rain stung against the window, the sea hushed, the pine trees sighed, the wind made a melancholy moaning in the cracks of the weather boards, down the chimney, and through the hole in the corner of the wardrobe. Malfred sighed, grateful, comfortable; it seemed that the prowler had gone. No one had broken into the house. She could see through the half-opened door into the alcove bedroom. The house was undisturbed. She was alone once again. She turned on her side, facing away from the window, closed her eyes, and fell asleep.

part three

•

THE STONE

·20·

THE METAPHOR OF SLEEP "knitting up the raveled sleeve of care" is neither hopeful nor exact. It describes a synthesis of care, the creation of a body of care existing on its own; one that can be touched and worn, used to keep out the weather, world weather and heart weather, all without banishing care itself. Would it not be more comforting for the many who are not Shakespeare if sleep were to destroy rather than knit up the ravelings? Sleep, one has always hoped, will make everything simple. Malfred could not have described her retreat to Karemoana as an attempt to make life and its care more simple, though the longing for simplicity was there, as it is always when a man or woman has reached middle age, for then the desire is to "autumn-clean" one's life—a kind of dry-cleaning where one does not expose the material to boisterous washday treatment, including hanging out the past in broad daylight, but to a gentle, careful removal of stains while pampering and preserving the material. There's no desire to begin again, to hang new curtains on the windows, buy new furniture; the old and used are convenient enough, and friendlier; but there's so much that is not wanted any more, that does not matter now, that has no meaning or of which the meaning is forgotten.

In middle age, this longing for simplicity swamps like a great wave that when it returns to the open sea does not bear away the flotsam of fifty-three years on earth; it merely makes itself and its power known, then retreats, leaving its own special jetsam; it doesn't care; nothing cares; neither do cares care, being knitted by grandmotherly dreams in sleep in the night, and during the day in fantasies; knitted, re-knitted into comfortable shawls, like the faded garments made for the refugees because—how will they tell the difference, having been so long cold and hungry?

Nor does emptiness, the clean sweep brought about by death, bring the simplicity longed for. For years Malfred's mother had lain within her life, aching like a tooth or tree stump. She had stayed far longer than the mothers of most of Malfred's friends and acquaintances. She had stayed so long that her role had become fictional, while Malfred had begun to live her own auto-biography, consoling herself that so-and-so, in history, had cared for her mother (remembering, too, that historical daughters were capable of murder as well as of loving care). This identification and concern during the conventionally "blossoming" years of her life, with another human being who was not the conventional mate, gave a fragmentation to Malfred's mind. Sometimes when she saw a woman passing who seemed to be the same age as herself, to wear similar clothes, who might, in other circumstances, have been her, Malfred had the impulse to call out to her, "Wait! Wait!" as if she were calling to herself or some part of herself. Then, if she saw the woman get into a car and be driven away by a man whom she had never seen, she would stare after them with a mixture of curiosity and intimacy, while from somewhere in her mind a thought, like a comet, flashed to the man, branding him as *her* husband; and then, as comets do, the thought flashed on, "disintegrating quietly into light."

The View of Malfred's life had been so long arranged with her mother in the foreground that her mother's death, though it set the View free, also left a hollow in the earth where the familiar tooth or tree stump had been removed, and where it was now too late for any other object to grow; perhaps the space resembled not so much a hollow as one of those disused mine shafts that are in a short time overgrown with weeds (noxious weeds) and grass, and where children and other small helpless animals, alike in their enjoyment of wilderness, choose to play, and falling, are trapped or die in the deep, dark, narrow shaft that penetrates to the center of the earth. No one would guess, from the atmosphere of desolation, neglect, doom, that surrounds the shaft, that here treasure was once mined, polished, displayed, cared for.

It may have been that Malfred's passion to paint the View and her interest in painting were being used by her in the last struggle for simplicity. It need not have been the last ally, yet such is the panic that often follows or accompanies middle age, a feeling of the draining away, like the release of a final afterbirth, of all resources, that many events, hopes and alliances of that period are felt to be the last. A woman in middle age looks inward to snatch at and rescue the desirable parts of herself; a man also looks and snatches, but he looks outward and his desperate capture is another human being, a woman—his wife, a mistress.

The poet's dream:

untroubling and untroubled here I lie
the grass beneath, above the vaulted sky,

two elements enclosing and comforting the tired body, could give the longed-for simplicity, if the dream were painted, if Malfred, staring from the window of her new home on a bright morning, should there ever be another morning, were able to ignore all irrelevant movement, color, form, and transfer to the blank rectangle of paper or canvas, almost as if she had mixed her vision with a chemical concentrate of mind—the sea, earth, sky alone. And if she framed this View, captured it, defined it by setting it (as it was long her habit to do) as seen through windows, doorways, so that when the picture itself was framed it became a kind of double-capture, a View within a View, double-burning, a double definition, then would not the expanse of untroubled color pour into her heart, bearing away, like the dreamed-of but unreliable tide, the irrelevance, the complexity, the personal flotsam of fifty-three years? She had thought it would be this way and that is why, sleeping, she showed none of the fear that haunted her throughout the storm. Her face was without pretense, without the waking muster of attack, disguise, fortitude, that make living into a war that ends only with sleep or death and of which the victor has never been decided. Nothing, no one wins. The forces of attack and defense are drawn from the same army!

And now the handiwork, the needlework, the tapestries, the knitting, are being patterned by sleep in the "room two inches behind the eyes," and the dream-signals come easily, in pictures and words. (For do not the cripples plot always to trip the dancers, the dumb extort their never-ending blackmail from the eloquent, those restricted to the spy hole view of their life break down the door into panoramic seeing?)

For all attain the goal, in the end, though their victory and reward may stay always in the room behind the eyes, unknown to all but themselves, or not even to themselves, to their consciousness, but perhaps to their body only—their skin (a twitch in the dream as the goal is reached, a cold sweat on the forehead as the cupboard opens to reveal the monster, a cry or groan that no one hears; a movement from side to side—window to wall or wall to window—that none see, or if seeing, interpret as a dream-message).

Now Malfred is lying asleep dreaming, her pictures set before her, her New View unfolding without hindrance, an island canvas that tries to make some pattern of her life. No one is going to mourn greatly when she dies. Her rhythm of people is monotonous and in many ways meaningless. Instead of Mother, Father, Wilfred, Lucy, Graham, the Art Society, the remembered teachers at the High School, she might just as well chant the anonymity of tinker, tailor, soldier (pausing a moment here), sailor, rich man, poor man, beggar man, thief, doctor, lawyer, merchant, chief; or quote the procession that goes with her to the grave as the procession to Widdicombe Fair—Bill Brewer, Jan Stewer, Peter Gurney, Peter Davey, Dan'l Whiddon, Harry Hawke. . . . Or, with the people banished, leaving only a hint of their flavor —salt, pepper, mustard, vinegar, for memory to skip to, and trip—where? What was the essence of Mother, Father, Wilfred, Lucy, Graham? And what was the essence of the most important person on the list, of her whose memory, like the old gray mare, would carry the others to Widdicombe Fair, and whose memory would in the end be seen in a dream sitting down to write its will, and then it would die, and then when the wind blew cold "on the moor of a night," the memory, like the old gray mare, would appear ghastly white? Whose essence, skipped and tripped over, burdened with an assortment of people clinging one to the other on the way to their destination, set in the gravewide words of the song,

All along, down along, out along lea.

Would there ever be a more extensive View than that given to a ghost,

All along, out along, down along, lea?

But whose essence?

·21·

MY ESSENCE. MINE. THERE'S no going back from the word "mine"; spoken, it is sprung, is born, cannot be killed. But who will claim the essence if I do not? It will be trampled at last by the ghost of the old mare as she roams "ghastly white," "all along, down along, out along lea," it will be dispersed as wide as wide as the View, and I do not want it to be dispersed, I want it framed, View within View, double-burning, therefore I claim it aloud, it is my essence, it is more important than shadow or odor or color of Mother, Father, Wilfred, Lucy, Graham. If I were to paint it I would apply all the rules of perspective, proportion, shading, color; my materials would be the best; but as I say this I remember that I've a New View of the world, and my New View must include my own essence, the pebble-core and simplicity of it.

Who am I, then? Where do I creep, crippled, or fly, dancing? I could put my hand over my life, obliterating it, disposing of it as I would an insect; there's no reason why others should not do this also, for I haven't cried out, "Save Me, Save Me," until tonight, when there's no one to hear me. All my life there has been someone within listening distance of me; I have been eavesdropped for fifty-three years, from my first heartbeat before I was born, all through my life; listening, listening to my lectures, at the Art Society, at school, at home; and all those years I never thought to cry "Save Me, Help, Help!" I planned for my future. In my first year of teaching when the insurance man called on me to describe the perils of retirement without what he called "something laid by," I acted swiftly, signed documents, arranged for deductions from my salary, to provide for myself when I turned fifty. Not the retiring age, the agent explained, but a *milestone*. Not half-way between birth and death, for few people reached their hundredth year with the honor of getting a telegram from the Queen or King, of being described (during the party in the Old Men's or Old Women's Home) as—what praise! —having such an endowment of breath that the blowing out simultaneously of one hundred candles left spare breath for the more important purpose of staying alive; of being asked to give advice to those who wished to live long enough to be an inmate of an Old Man's or Old Woman's Home, blowing out one hundred candles, getting a telegram from the Queen or King, being asked to give advice to those who . . . A dangerous circuit to be trapped in, in spite of the icing on top of the cake and the one hundred candles and thirty-six thousand five hundred and twenty-five mornings!

I repeat that the insurance agent looked on fifty as a "round age," a "milestone," a time to "take stock" to count assets, face liabilities. Not only insurance agents think this way of fifty years. Poets do, preparing for it every ten years from their twentieth year—"On this day I complete my twentieth, thirtieth, etc. year."

There is seldom mention given by insurance agents or poets of the need for someone to eavesdrop the cry "Help, Help! Save Me," when the fiftieth (thirtieth, twentieth) year is reached.

But let me turn widdershins into the "room two inches behind the eyes" (crippled, a dancer; dumb, made eloquent) and see what it is I wish to be saved from. I left my family, my home-town, my island, my climate. (My spring! with its pussy willows, its weed on the ponds, green weed growing so fast its growth flashes across the surface overnight. I say "flashes," but there's nothing to prove its flashing; not any more; who cares to keep watch all night in the hope of witnessing a firefly weed growing on a stagnant pond in the middle of a swampy paddock?) No matter. I left that world to come to this foreign land, this island with its giant patriarchal pohutukawas dipping their red Christ-mas beards in the bright blue waters of the gulf, to this white house on the hill where the former owner died surrounded by her leatherbound, pocket editions of the poets and her Christmas Omar Khayyáms (I've counted three). I came here to a night of storm, a state of siege. What besieges me? Who besieges me? It is not leatherbound, pocket editions of poets though I, who all my life have insisted on accommodating shadows, have space to spare in myself for the shadow (my share of her shadow) of the retired teacher who spent her time with Elizabeth Barrett Browning in a "battered caravanserai of nights and days," having "fears that she might cease to be," "tired with all these crying for restful death," sitting in a basket chair at the front door watching the fantails feeding in the black hearts of the flax flowers, and finally having the satisfaction or alarm of knowing that her fears were justified, and that "restful death" had come.

What is it then that besieges me? Who is it?

Father?

Mother?

Lucy?

Graham?

Roland?

Wilfred?

The Old Girls, the Art Society, myself?

What is it, who is it?

Tonight I will solve this mystery. Sometimes I have thought that I will turn against everyone I have known to claim from them the part of the essence of me that they possess, to fit together the claimed parts into a pattern of wholeness that I shall value more than endowment as security for old age and death. Perhaps I should take Mother, Father, Graham, Lucy, Wilfred, the Art Society, place them together in a special extracting machine, hold myself beneath the outlet and there receive the parts of myself that have been stolen, snatched by them, in or out of my presence, for both presence and absence are dangers; there are no guarantees that the body, being visible, can prevent the theft of its essence, just as there is no guarantee that the invisible body gathers its precious essence about it, out of the way of the distant scavengers. It may be that a person, in absence, is more thoroughly scavenged. I wonder, now, what parts of me are being seized, held to the light, snipped, trimmed, polished, gilded, reshaped, fouled, adorned by the people I have known? How can I arm myself with a New View, a New Life, when my Self, the armory, is threatened not only by my past and its inhabitants but by these immediate presences that besiege me in my white house on the hill?

Now I make my picture. The room is windowless, warm. Saying good-bye to sensations of night, storm, fear, to the sound of knocking and the imprisoning sea, I go in. The floor is patterned with the kind of squares that belong to everyone's memory— gingham dresses (photos in the Gardens, in front of the Begonia House, on the Japanese bridge), tablecloths, tea towels, of games played with a hierarchy of tall kings and bishops or with squat wrinkled draughts; or simply memories of squares of light and shadow—linoleum on the kitchen floor, in maze shapes with no entrance or exit, handkerchiefs, squares in the hand, on the clothesline flying shapes distorted by movement and light; square lawns, drainage grills, ancient courtyards seen only in the imagination.

I sit down in one of the golden squares, smoothing my golden brown hair in its plaits, knowing that the color of the floor highlights the burnished tint of my hair. I sit surrounded by dreams that, unfolded, will make pictures. I have a feeling of peace, of happiness. My hands begin to clasp and unclasp themselves, waiting, eager to begin the unfolding of each dream. All my past dreams are there. I see the labels Father, Mother, Graham, Lucy, Wilfred, the tall letters, tall as winter chimneys in other lands where winter is too cold for open windows, fireless rooms, and a walk in the frost on a clear morning with the haze ribboned along the horizon. Flames burst from the spires of the letters. There must be a fire at the foot, at the floor there, I think, and I get up from my golden square and walk from letter to letter, as if I walked from chimney to chimney or pillar to pillar, in a cloister of dreaming, seeking the fire; but I cannot find it, therefore I return to my golden square, and sit quietly while the names form, the names of my places—the frost and fire-split rocks of Kurow, the green and silver shingle-swirl and sigh of Waitaki, the cattle dust, dry grass of Waiareka.

Unpinning my plaits I say to myself, I am Malfred Signal, I am fifty-three years old. I was twenty-eight when war broke out, I have in my memory the personal irrelevances that make each year of history a different age for each person, not one year but millions each seen through the eyes of one person here, there, north, south, east, west. The thought of so many years, the human burden of millions of years set within the so cleanly dismissed three hundred and sixty-five days, of time unrecorded, lived by people I shall never know or imagine, makes me feel helpless, like a child again when I had not the right arithmetic even to count the linoleum squares on the kitchen floor. I begin to wind my plaits in a stiff wire of self-control about my head, and their glossy brown changes to the accustomed gray, and my lips are set once more in my fifty-third year, like a shape set inside a stone, and once again I am certainly what the girls at school used to call me—not to my face, but I knew—*old fossil*. I am an old fossil, and I sit here, an old fossil, in my golden square, still quite happy, my childhood and the First World War forgotten, except that—Oh! I'm remembering that all my uncles had moustaches—and some of my aunts, too, had a moustache!

All is well, dream-room philosophy, cripple to dancer, dumb to eloquent, though I was never dumb, suits me until suddenly I am struck a blow that sends me leaping to my feet, running to the door (it is locked now) and crying, "Help, Help," and it is as if I were awake again in the white house on the hill with the wind and the sea outside and the prowler knocking at my door, myself besieged. I wonder what has caused such sudden fear in me. Then I realize that in my dream-room two inches behind the eyes there are no shadows. No shadows! But everything has shadows, always: objects, people, plants, little dogs, plaits, uncles have shadows, their moustaches have shadows; aunts have shadows, lovers, mothers, fathers, even the dead have shadows— surely?—and the shadows stand or lie strongly wiving or husbanding their shape, in the only true eternal unity, fitness, completeness. Then as I struggle to escape from this shadowless room I notice that though I can see, as if I were out in the world in daylight, the room, in fact, is without light, is sealed from light, and that faint sound I hear as of a moaning wind that rises and dies away and seems to probe with its fingers against the walls and door of the dream-room, is Light, trying to get in. "Only let me in," Light is saying. "Let our armies in, that we might each stand guard over our chosen shape; only let me in that I may bring the armies of shadow to guard the shapes of your dreaming; shadows that at noon are a broken cloud, blot, clod, wrapped shape, huddled parcel, that at twilight go walking the world, tall as the sky."

Then the sound changes to a moan, a cringing, whining cry that I never believed could be made by Light; it seems to have lost all pride—Light that stayed once in its supremacy, its royal kingdom, to have become a beggar in the shadowless room of dreaming!

"You, Malfred Signal," it seems as if the Light is saying, "you were always the champion of shadows, you with your colleagues were the sole champions; why, then do you not let me in to your dream-room that your dreams may be shaded? Remember the house in the picture, the red roof, the chimney, the smoke coming out of the chimney to mingle with the snow-threatened sky, the tree exactly half-way between red wall and brown fence, the tree complete with shadow? The red gate for the children to swing on—the gate with its picketed shadow, the children with their pinafored shadow? Remember the footpath outside? The people walking along the street, each secure, street and people, in his shadow? You do not know how thankful I, Light, felt that in you and your colleagues we had champions of our morning, noon and twilight cause. And now you would exclude me, deny me the practice of my skill. How eagerly throughout the years I have listened to your indirect praise of me. Oh no, you did not sing, 'Hail, Holy Light.' Your praises were more subtle and practical, you gave two generations of schoolgirls an obsession with shading, with shadows. And now when you retire and go to live in your white house on the hill on an island, intent on seeing, painting, a New View of the world and of yourself, when, sleeping, you enter the room two inches behind the eyes, the room that all your life you have been afraid to enter while awake, now you exclude all light, and therefore all shade and shadow. Why?"

Accused, I put my hands over my face, though there is no light of accusation to shine on me and hurt my eyes. I try to explain, talking aloud, that I have no control over the arrangement and furnishing of my dream-room, but I know my protests are useless, the sound outside continues, the light snuffles, whimpers, roars, now a dog, now a horse—I see its flying mane, its wild, fiery-red eyes, the hooves shod with light. I am oppressed by the awful cavity of this dream-room—it seems suddenly like a hollow where a tooth has been, the gashed earth where the tree has been torn away. How I wish the Light would come in, the door open, the walls break apart; Light step in with all the accustomed gallantry of morning, with shadow, like an opera cloak thrown carelessly over its shoulders, highwayman Light come to rob the dark to provide for the shapes it will shine upon!

I decide to stand near the door. I know that here and now, in sleep, I have arrived at my New View of the world, that in spite of the noise of Light wanting to get in, its battering, hammering, pleading, I must deny it; I must face my New View of the world without its help; I must paint the objects, people, plants, the islands in a burning wholeness of shape that is deprived of shade. I have no choice now. I have no control over the Light's entry. Here, darkness makes everything noon. The generosity of darkness is heaped upon itself to form the deprived, shadowless noon.

There's a smell of burning. The letters on the named dreams are surely on fire. Again, I feel that I cannot stay longer in this dream-room. Will no one let me out? Could Light help, out there, sweeping with its lantern, smashing with its hooves on the door? "Help, Help! Save me, save me." Oh, why did I not cry "Help Help Save me save me" when I was born fifty-three years ago—or perhaps I did cry it and no one heard because no one knew my language; they thought my cry was the cry of life!

But who is this entering the dream-room? It is my father. He wears mountaineering clothes, his ice axe and rope slung across his slight shoulders. See, the left shoulder still droops, his eye still twitches, he is the father I knew and not the handsome stone man that stands overlooking the Cape of Matuatangi. He has entered the room without opening the door; this is in approved dream or ghost style. He has walked in as a wave walks into the darkness, except that his body is contained in one whole, unlike a wave that scatters itself on impact with darkness or light, with shore, with human skin. Yet, if I observe closely, I will see that my father has indeed distributed himself about the room, he is not the whole being I imagined; the man whom citizens have fashioned in stone, in hero stance; he has behaved like a bubble in the dream-room; there is nothing I can grasp of him that does not belong to another person, age or place; even snowflakes leave a stain where they have fallen. My father who, in spite of his teaching, his good works, his friends, was a solitary man, has gone without protest (as he, a mild, gentle creature would do) into the area of universal belonging, where the known arithmetic does not work, where division is not division, but what it is I can't explain or find out.

There is a house on the hill, with granny's bonnets and marigolds growing on both sides of the long winding path; it's a big family house where the family is poor and cannot afford to pay the rent, and at the end of the month they come to my father's office to give him what they have saved. It is never the full rent; their debt mounts. The landlord asks my father to give the family notice of eviction; but my father has said no, he will make up the unpaid difference each month from his own pocket, until times improve and the family can afford to pay their rent.

"How do you know they will be able to pay?" the landlord demands. "Or that times will improve?"

My father has brown eyes, and though in the childhood rhyme brown eyes are pick-the-pie, in my father they are faith and trust.

"Times will improve," he replies.

His prophecy is correct. One day the mother comes into the office of Signal and Signal with a purseful of money. Her old, black handbag has a torn lining. One of the five-pound notes has to be rummaged for down inside this torn lining, near the rotting cardboard spine of the bag, down among crumbs, fluff, a dome, a small spiral shell from a broken string of beads, a button, and more fluff.

"You're a gentleman, Mr. Signal," the woman says, with exactly the right tone that implies my father is a gentleman; not many men are gentlemen (including the landlord who wanted to evict the family). Also, there is the slightest hint that this fat little woman with the worn, black handbag with the broken brass clasp and the ragged lining, is a *gentlewoman*.

And then, when the receipt is given—"I know I can trust you, Mr. Signal, but I must have a receipt!" (A receipt to this family is as important as a diploma.) The woman sighs thankfully.

"You are a gentleman, Mr. Signal!"

She and my father talk then—about native birds, she puts food out for the little ringeyes and there's a tui in her garden—about native trees—leather leaf, koromiko, ribbonwood, manuka, native beech, plants above and below the snow line, mountain orchids, daisies, lilies; the woman proud, though she cannot explain why, to be talking about plants that are "native" and not commonplace, worldwide, not *English*. ("My mother came out with the first settlers, Mr. Signal!")

When at last the woman goes home to her drab domestic routine, trying once again to make ends meet, she has taken with her a share of my father that I never knew or held, because I was Malfred Signal, simply the daughter of Francis Henry Signal;

because I was not a little fat woman with a black handbag with torn lining and fluff and a button and a dome and a spiral shell from a broken string of beads lying side by side with the five-pound notes.

Oh, there are so many qualifications for owning people! Being a daughter, a son, husband, wife, lover, are not always the most suitable qualifications for possessing part of a near relative. Somewhere in or out of Matuatangi, in the North Island or South Island or the world, there is a family of children, grown-up now, whose mother and father may be long dead, but who tell *their* children, as a bedtime story, the story of "old Mr. Signal" (yet my father was never old), of "old Mr. Signal" who many, many years ago—so long ago that the telling might qualify for "Once upon a time"—saved them from being turned out of their home. The home will be described, the granny's bonnets and marigolds along the path, the number of rooms, the places where the children used to play—with asides like, "He's your uncle Mervin, that's your cousin Mona"; the landlord will be painted as the villain; the rescuing knight, "old Mr. Signal" moves in and out of the story, as its theme.

It is strange that without our being aware of it, when my father died, my mother died, Lucy married, Graham married, when I was appointed to my first teaching post, whenever the name of Signal was news, a family (many families, for this woman was not the only one to whom my father gave hope, and part of himself that we never received) would exchange remarks among themselves,

"That is one of the Matuatangi Signals."

(How we love to attach people to their distinctive places!)

"Old Mr. Signal was such a gentleman."

(Saying this in a tone which implies sharing of my father's gentlemanly qualities.)

But what can *I* say of him? I never saw him in this way.

Now, in the dream-room my father has given no evidence that he has seen me; but why should he? He has two arms, two hands, ten fingers; yet I do not see him glance at his left arm, start with surprise, smile at it, exclaim,

"Oh, it is you, my left arm! Where have you been, how did you come to be here in this dream-room?"

Am not I, as my father's daughter, in the same category as his left arm, right arm, ten fingers? I am there always. There can never be an amputation of me. Yet, it is strange to think that if the little fat woman with the ragged handbag were to come into this room now, my father, recognizing her, would welcome her, ask after her health, her family. If any of his former clients or pupils were here, he would greet them; or members of the Council, citizens of Matuatangi whom he may recognize but who were not close friends. Because I am his daughter, he neither sees me nor speaks to me; and now he is gone, carrying no awareness of me, absorbed only in Council matters, stone seats that must be inscribed, native trees that must be planted and cared for, scholarships that must be founded, the rent arrears of the poor that must be paid from his own pocket "until times improve."

Then there are the mountains beyond the Southern Lakes where, though he went with parties from the mountaineering club, or prefects and sixth-formers from school, no one could follow him; there he was alone. I think he has gone now to those mountains beyond the Southern Lakes to explore, to name new peaks. He knew men who died in the Alps. They were young men, University teachers and students. No one can set foot above the snow line without being reminded of the youthful dead who, wishful legend tells, are purified by dying in white wastes, where the winds that buried their bones in the snow are mountain winds, first from the sky and the clouds, untainted by men, cities; winds born of snow, bearing snow, returning to snow. So the dead Bill, Frank, Norman, Harold, lie luminously boned and souled, enshrined with their promise. Every year there was a sacrifice to the Alps. I remember my father used to talk passionately of men who had "died in the Alps"; there was always a special silence in his manner after he said, "He was killed in the Alps—remember?" And people would remember and you could almost see in their eyes their private journeying to glaciers and snow fields, their contemplation of luminously purified souls and bones; their momentary sharing of the vision, bathing in their own imagined purity; then the flash of envy as, with a mixture of reluctance and eagerness, they blinked back to their impure benighted lives.

"A frightful tragedy," they would say, dismissing Bill, Frank, Norman, Harold.

They would talk then of the thoughtlessness of the inexperienced mountaineer, the cost of rescue work, of the reasons that men climb mountains and die in them.

I remember that one of the girls in the English class used to recite a poem she had learned in private elocution lessons. Her face assumed a similar expression of contemplation of death in purity, though she spoke of sheep, not men!

Sheep that have died on the mountains,
These their bones,

Here where the falcons hover
High among stones:

. . .

Strayed they, weary and sick? They fell
High among stones:
The dawn heard their cries, and the night:
These their bones.

Perhaps, in this country, sheep and men are so close, so dependent one upon the other that in their mountain deaths there is an intermixture of sanctity, the splintered gray bones uncovered in the snow, lying among the golden wirestalks of snowgrass growing up through the bones' private crevasses, have lost their outer artificial layer and label—sheep, man—and found, in their purification by snow, their common company of bone?

My father has gone from the room now. I have seen photographs of him in those books written from time to time by mountaineers; books with maps, big print, many photographs of men camping, men in snow, men in mountain huts. Why do these expedition photographs date so quickly? My father, who never looked "modern" already has an Edwardian appearance in those photographs. Is it because snow, never changing, casts upon men who have been photographed in it, all the burden of change and time? Last year's snow is as white as this year's, but last year's suit and shoes and hat and the man wearing them have aged doubly.

I think that in my life I have drawn most from that region where my father explored and none of us could follow. Oh Karemoana, flatly fashioned, how cobbled you are with your small hills drawn together by tangled threads of scrub and gorse, and not a mountain, not a mountain in the eye! I think that I could take the Southern Alps, described as a "mountain chain"—a chain of stones, of snow, of rock—described as "the backbone" of the South Island—a backbone of stones—I think that I could thread the peaks together as if they were the spiral shells from the broken string of beads, and wear them forever, like pearls— though whose disease, my treasure—about my throat.

· 22 ·

HERE IS MY MOTHER now, she also is not seeing or speaking to me, for I have been a part of her. A woman of shadows, she does not suit this shadowless world. When she died, she died of a particular disease, in a particular place, but dying and death are not parochial, they invade, spread, pursue an ironic policy of "lebensraum," so that when I see my mother here before me I cannot tell from what disease she died. She appears ghostly, ill, even to her fingernails and hair that are such determined growths, scratching at the eyes of the soil, lying in plaits of growth in the dark, after the heart has stopped beating. Let me look at my mother closely. She has long gray hair, the growth thin, revealing the bones of her skull, the old-woman pigmentation of her skin, those brown maps that appear, like a geographer's vegetation map, on the skin of elderly people—in the corners of their eyes, at the top of their forehead near the hairline, about the ankles, on the backs of the hands. On the upper arms, the golden brown marks (tundra to plateau to savannah to plain to rain forest) change to red like old scorch marks that also appear on the breasts, near the underarms, making the colorless hairs seem like a patch of burned plain.

The skin of my mother's face has worn thin, as if something—days or years—has trodden it, rubbed it; perhaps it suffers from the friction of being upright in air. Her nose is all bone, the mean coat-hanger shape of the nose in an anonymous skull. Her eyes retain their color, their composition as eyes. She is dressed in the costume she wore the day of my father's funeral. It is smart and neat, yet it does not fit her old-woman shape; she might just as well have worn her shroud.

As I watch her walk across the room I feel the usual depression at the nondescriptness of her, at the nondescriptness of most people, even those known and dear. It would be different if all people were so, but they are not. There are those who have distinction in death; if they came to this room I could admire them, feel satisfaction at their singularity, but I cannot do this with my mother or with my father; for I see him not as the handsome stone man set on a windswept cape overlooking the town and harbor, but as the slight, shy man with the limp, and though this appearance has its individuality, the core of distinction is not there, or I cannot see it.

How ordinary my mother is! I never thought otherwise. She is like grass withered on the side of a country road where no people, only wind and dust walk and telegraph poles stand linking wires, moans and messages. She is like any old fragment from any old human being. That fierce expression in her eyes, like a hawk's eye when it sees a rabbit or small bird on the plain, is born of her knowledge of her drabness even in death, marks her permanent lookout from a suitable deathly peak for the bright wing of distinction flashing by. Oh, she is so drab, so nondescript, that her predatory eyes would seize, snap up any individuality from any object she chanced to see. Even my own being, here in this room, is not safe from her greed. She is like the sun leaning for sight of a mountain lake to suck up its darkness and shining water.

But the sun has distinction!

Also, there is no sun to suck lakes here, in this room, and so my mother, for whom I gave up so many years of my life, is walking drab, commonplace, in a matter-of-fact way, as if this dream-room were a bank or an office or a supermarket where, after all, in her life and in her death, she did not find the special bargain she was looking for.

She goes now, without a shadow, and as I watch her I am reminded how much of the burden of human flesh is shared by shadows, and what a blow it is for the flesh to have no shadow: a literal blow, as if the body, walking the earth, stepped suddenly upon a plank of darkness that leapt up striking its victim be-tween the eyes. A shadow is such a natural, right possession to walk and sit with, to lie with, to make love with (two people, two shadows, four lovers). We walk with our shadows as a cat walks with pride in its tail; when a cat sits, see how it curls its tail neatly about its body as if to say, "This is my tail, see how it suits me, encloses me, acts as my boundary when I sit or walk or spring or sleep." Man, without his shadow, as the primitive peoples believed, is robbed of his essence, of his first and last company and friend that follows him even to his grave, stays with him, sleeping, until he is dust, then as dust-shadow to dust flies with him in the eyes and breath of the wind round and round the world. Oh, I think now that I understand my need to learn and teach the art of shading; I think that my concern with fire shovels and their shadows was not wholly the crime that some may have thought it to be.

My mother looks back over her shoulder, and her eyes' hunger says, "I am nothing, I am lanolin and white sheets with the laundry mark, like the number of a convicted prisoner stamped in blue in one corner, and yet even the laundry mark is not my identity, for the sheets have been to several laundries and the numbers are so overprinted that no distinct one emerges. I am nothing but what I am, that is, my decaying body belongs to me, my two arms, hands, ten fingers and—" Mother is pointing wildly at me— "my daughter Malfred Signal, she belongs to me. Malfred, the lanolin, please!"

"Yes, Mother."

"Please, dear!"

"Is your back hurting? Would you like more pillows? I've learned a new comfortable way to stack them. No, Mother, I've not been sketching by the Old Mill or around the Cape or at the Waitaki mouth. You remember the doctor said you were to have constant company. No, Mother, you are not in danger but you must have constant companionship. Ship is the state of."

"But where's my shadow, Malfred? Someone's taken away my shadow! You were always such a clever girl with shading and shadows. I remember when you were little and Auntie Marion came to stay and you drew her portrait and you were so careful about the shading; we all admired the shading more than the portrait. Such thick, black lines as if you had worked with charcoal or a carpenter's pencil but it was only BB wasn't it? All those artist's tools that are so full of mystery! Tempera, what is tempera, Malfred? My memory is not as reliable as it used to be. And I remember you used to bring home those pretty stones from the creek and put them on the mantelpiece and draw them, all with their shadow; mottled blue stones, blue with the cold, you said; some were fossils, with shell shapes inside them. You drew them, all with their shadow. No one else in the family had the gift like you. We tried, didn't we, Malfred, to find where you got it from?

"She must get it from somewhere, everyone said. But there was nothing we could point to, though the early settlers were so clever, especially the women with their fingers, and your grandmother was clever with her fingers, though she wasn't one of the earliest settlers. Not one of those Jane Cressey, Jane Seymour snobs! The women in those days made pictures from shells, from hair, and leftover strands of cotton. They worked tapestry—tea roses, deer, and highland cattle; their cooking was full of imagination. If cakes could be permanent they would be hung on the walls of homes and in art galleries as a National Art—you've said so yourself, Malfred, haven't you? All those framed melting moments, Pavlova cakes, Scottish pikelets, Spanish cream, butterfly kisses—all interesting new collages. . . .

"But we grew tired of trying to find out where you got it from, Malfred, and then we were jealous of you because you had it. Once when you were small, you came home from school with a little spaniel dog, a mongrel, may I say, and it stayed by you, and wouldn't let you out of its sight, and we said, 'Where'd you

197

get it?' and you said, 'I didn't see where it came from. It just followed me.'

"We thought you might have stolen it! We thought, too, that you might have stolen your talent for art from one of us. And then we forgot to wonder. Your father died. Soon you were grown up. Then I was ill. You were always first in the class for shading!"

"Stop it, Mother. Stop saying that!"

"Why dear? I thought you liked shading. You always liked shading. Why, I remember . . ."

"Stop it, Mother!"

"All right, Mally. I'll stop if you want me to. I shouldn't like to do anything you don't want me to do. I was like that with your father, too. I always bowed to his wishes. He was a gentle man. Do you know, Mally, that when people are at the guillotine waiting to be executed they bow their head, they bow, just as I used to do with my wishes. But what is it you don't like me saying about shading, Mally? You were always so clever at it, measuring and planning and filling in. Where's *my* shadow, Mally? Mally!"

"You don't have a shadow now, Mother, because there's no sun. Never any more sun nor morning."

"But you can make me one, Mally. Please! You with all your pencils, crayons, paints and your flair for painting; and if you've got tired of shading, perhaps you can run me a shadow up on the machine, putting a stitch in it here and there to make it stay and fit."

"Oh, Mother, you can't make shadows that way. They have to grow out of your body. You need the sun, light."

"Wouldn't something bright do—one of those yellow flowers, a marigold, a sunflower, even one of those deep red antirrhinums? Or a buttercup? Isn't there a substitute for the sun, for light? I thought that these days there was a substitute for everything."

"But you're not living in these days, Mother, you're not living in any day, you're dead."

"Never any more sun, never any more sun nor morning. When I was lying in my bed at home, Malfred, and morning came, I could see the sun shining on those tall, white, autumn lilies, the ones with the yellow center. They were just tall enough to look in the window. Oh how I miss my room, Mally. I miss the window sill so much, the part where the wood had come off and where the paint peeled from the window sash just after your father died, and it was never repainted; that streak of raw wood underneath; and the hooks in the window sash, for opening the window; houses don't have hooks like that nowadays, Mally, and the windows don't have blinds like ours, not navy; they're all venetians now. And we had tassels, Mally. Tassels! And those tiny tacks pinning the blind to the roller, and the tear, streaked with daylight, at the bottom of the blind, and the two 'dead' blinds, that wouldn't go up.

"How the dew flashed on the autumn lilies! I could see the mist lying over the town on an autumn morning; a gray mist laced with light shining in the back door of the clouds and not quite reaching the front door of the world; and the mist used to give me such a strange dull feeling that I was living in Matuatangi, in our house, in my bedroom, sick in bed, that yesterday had been, and tomorrow would come, and today was here, all in such a strange, dull way—a restful dullness—but a feeling that we used to have when we were children and stayed away from school and went outside in the daylight, and it seemed as if everyone in the world had gone somewhere else, somewhere more exciting and interesting, that staying away had been a terrible mistake, but nothing could be done about it, it had to be lived through, all the long, long day. But being in bed was such a heavy dullness, too, as if it would need more than one, two, twenty, a thousand people to shift it, as if the lightly floating mist were the weight of the world and there were no shoulders to bear the weight. I express it now, Mally, as I would never have expressed it before, but it's how I *felt* then. I felt sick and dull, dull like lukewarm washing water, like bananas gone black around the edges, not because there was something wrong with them but because that is how bananas go when you peel them and leave them; or like apples gone brown when someone has taken two or three bites and thrown the apple away.

"Lying in bed I could see so much of the town. I could see the dark red of the railway station and the engine sheds and the heaps of dusty coal in the yards. I could see the smoke from the mill chimney, and the big boot of the shoe shop, and the signs in daylight, empty of color and bright light. I could see the trees in the street, and in early spring the soft green haze that surrounds them, as if their leaves are part of the air before they become part of the tree; I mean the elm trees, Mally. And then I could hear all the necessary and unnecessary noises of Matuatangi—the train whistle, the shunting noises at the engine shed, the bell at the railway crossing, the children let out of school at playtime and lunchtime, the twelve o'clock mill whistle, the town clock striking each quarter hour; shouts and cries and barks and hoots and the whining of saws; and the sea, always the sea, our special green Matuatangi sea. My bones were so tired, Malfred, my body kept sinking into the sheets, and you always plumped the pillows so nicely for me, you were a born nurse, and you rubbed the meths into my back and powdered me with my baby powder, the sterilized kind, so that I would not get tetanus. My skin was so withered. I would put my face close to the sheet, to get used to it, and more used to it, and a small valley of my smell stayed under my pillow. I did not like my smell, Mally, it stayed too long with me, without changing, as if it said, 'Ha, Ha. I'm going all the way!'

"All the way.

"*All along, down along, out along lea.* Remember the song you used to sing about Tom Pearce? Your father was fond of that song, too, and when he sang he had a pleasant voice. What was it now? Tom Pearce, Tom Pearce, lend me your gray mare . . .

All along, down along, out along lea,
for I want for to go to Widdicombe Fair
with . . .

"Who were the men they went with to Widdicombe Fair? It was unselfish of Tom Pearce to lend the mare, don't you think? *All along, down along, out along lea.* You always tried to make my bed so comfortable, Mally, but there were lumps and blots that kept digging into my spine. My spine has crumbled away now. The only backbones left are the mountains and the stones. When I was a girl and a woman, they used to say that I walked, stood, and sat straight as a rod. That was my spine, Mally. Like a rod. Some of the girls in my day had curvature. Curvature of the spine.

"I lay in bed keeping my spine straight, in spite of the discomfort, and the sun shone from the autumn lilies into the room, back and forth, with the dust traveling upon it, like those brightly-winged birds that travel on the backs of golden wild animals in the jungle.

"The sun made shadows, Malfred. It gave me a shadow, too."

My mother is crying. There is nothing I can do for her now. She goes out of the windowless, sunless, shadowless room into her windowless, sunless, shadowless state of death.

I do not think, now, that it is my mother who has besieged me in the night and storm.

·23·

NOR DO I THINK that I am besieged by this man who comes into the room as if he fled from a storm. He is young, tall, well-built, with fair hair. He wears a soldier's uniform. If I were to try to identify him from this description alone, I might be deceived into supposing that he is Wilfred; but immediately when I think of Wilfred, I must search in my mind for any remains of him. I know that when a person is taken from the hazardous weather of being into the shelter of memory, he enters on the terms of memory alone, that is, as prey that will be devoured in the end. Fattened and garnished, like Hansel and Gretel, with witch attendants poking their fingers through the bars to see if the meal is "ready," he may stay unharmed for years, that is, unharmed by the final harm of oblivion, not by change, by time. What keepsake have I of Wilfred? How do I know that this man is or is not Wilfred? He has Wilfred's height, build, hair coloring, clothes— but these are common to so many young men! So many, too, share the inner furniture. How one longs for one among them to stand out, to startle with different height, build, hair coloring, clothes! The common pool; the interchange of spare parts; and no one notices: Ted, Bill, Frank, Harry, Peter, Dan'l, Wilfred. . . . It is especially hard to distinguish them now in their army uniform, all wearing the same wounds like ragged red medals over their hearts; they are like sheep now, dead in more sordid places than mountains, though their deaths, in these circumstances, in the snow, would reach the limits of impurity.

Or, perhaps, they are like the cattle in the poem,

The cattle are grazing
Their heads never raising,
There are forty feeding like one.

Feeding on their death?

It is easy to understand the argument that would abolish thirty-nine, and, for want of world space, keep the remaining one— head, heart of cattle, sheep or man.

When I search my memory I find that I have nothing of Wilfred alone, of his "essence." It is as if my memory deceived me into thinking it had taken photographs of Wilfred alone, and when I study the photographs I find Wilfred and the rhododendrons, Wilfred and the wool shed, Wilfred and Five Hills, Wilfred and the sheep, Wilfred and the Jubilee, Wilfred and his uncle, who climbed mountains with my father; Wilfred and the fernhouse; then, Wilfred and myself. If he knew, would he protest at my inability to isolate him, to give him his lonely place on a dais, throne, scaffold, or anywhere that man may stand alone in glory or guilt? Wilfred and I, Wilfred and Five Hills, Wilfred and the sheep! Only slightly less overwhelming than Miss Float's, "Here I am with Canterbury Cathedral," "Here with Dove Cottage, the Tower of London, Haworth Parsonage, Constable's Mill." Had Wilfred lived, would his memory contain as little of my essence? Would there not be my mother and I, my sister and I, my brother and I, the Jubilee and I, the Art Society, and—more subtle—my painting and I?

If I try the experiment of ignoring Wilfred, of staring closely at the wool shed, the sheep, Five Hills, the Jubilee, I realize with dismay that the image of Wilfred is not even necessary, that he is contained as much in the wool shed, Five Hills, the Jubilee (and myself?), the sheep, as he is in himself, that one cancels the other. On the other hand, if I were to blot out the wool shed, keeping the image of Wilfred alone, it is likely that, scanning him for identity, I should exclaim— "That is the wool shed, the wool shed of Five Hills Farm!"

These shufflings and confusions of memory must be reckoned with. The one exception to this mingling of identity is, strangely, the image of the time when Wilfred and I could be described as fusing identities. I'm thinking of the episode in the fernhouse. Here, in this room two inches behind the eyes, while I sleep, the memory is clearly illuminated, and those darknesses that are never seen or known or acknowledged in waking life, are clear, too; the memory of the fernhouse emerges untrimmed, untapered, burning to full height and shadow and strength; for we made love in the fernhouse, and I did not, as I need to remember that I did, turn Wilfred away or mock him but I loved him with my body and with my thoughts. It is hard to find words to describe it, for it has been described so many times with the eye of the writer looking at or away from the object; it has been described in trite ways or simple ways, as in the Biblical *He knew her, she knew him.* I cannot think of it in this way. Nor can I say dramatically, "Here in the fernhouse I surrendered to him, we were one." I have seen and heard all these phrases and none is right and clear, none is exact. I could say, "We made love," but that is too swift and general a statement, it robs me of my essence, of my having been myself, Malfred Signal, and of his having been himself, Wilfred.

Therefore, I will not try to describe it. Its place among the ferns and bush was right. It is elements—earth, air, fire, water— each time with a particular element in ascendance. There, it was water—creeks, drains, dew, stagnant pools, waterfalls, and finally, sea, sea bed, and what rest or temporary absence of restlessness lies on the sea bed. But seas dry up, the ferns in the fernhouses wither. Here in my dream-room, have not my memory and my desire embellished the story? All I may keep of that time in the fernhouse of Matuatangi Gardens is the knowledge that whatever happened, when my memory came to preserve the image of Wilfred and myself in the fernhouse, out of all the memory images recorded, it is in this that Wilfred and I preserve our essence, because however much I may distort it or dream it, we gave ourselves to each other, without thinking of the consequences—I do not mean the looming physical consequences, but those ruled by the deeper, more frightening facts of arithmetic: I have myself. I give myself. Therefore, I have nothing left. And because the condition of loving is that one withholds noth-

ing, not even a scrap of identity tied in the corner of a handker-
chief, to go on loving and obeying this condition is an act of
courage, at first; it becomes, later, an act of cunning, after one
has learned of the surprising rewards that lie in this new over-
turning of all the rules of arithmetic: I give equals I keep. Loses
keeps.

The final irony is that the phrase, *Finds keeps, loses weeps,* is
now applied in all its variations; with no easing of pain to the
finder or loser.

Loses keeps, loses weeps, finds keeps, finds weeps.

Now this young man in the soldier's uniform turns towards me.
I see his face. He is not Wilfred, or not the Wilfred I knew. Not
Wilfred and the Jubilee, Wilfred and Five Hills, Wilfred and
the sheep, Wilfred and the wool shed. Not Wilfred and I in the
fernhouse. It is another Wilfred, in another place, a snapshot I
do not keep; it is Wilfred and the war. I cannot even say, as he
stands without his shadow that might have retained some likeness to him, that he is my Wilfred and his war is Wilfred's war.

This soldier home from the wars (sand in his uniform, blood
over his heart, his face scarred and burned, his lips swollen,
suffering the cliché indignities in a way that distracts attention
from the invisible unremarkable horror) begins to speak to me.
Even if he were Wilfred he would not know me, this middle-aged
woman haunted by storm and knocking and the sea, and
everything in or out of the world wanting to get in. If this were
Wilfred he would say,

"Hello, Mall."

Mall! Like Pall Mall!

"Hello, Mally. Mally, I know we've been seeing a lot of each other—as things are, Mally . . ."

As things are!

"Perhaps we could manage life at Five Hills together. . . ."

One of the crimes of war is that the macabre shocking experiences it brings will shrivel the seed of originality until the withering shows itself even in a man's language. Hello, Mall. As things are. We've been seeing a lot of each other. One does not need war to help spill platitudes!

But now, Wilfred, looking directly at me, changes his tone, his words bursting like blisters from his lips,

"You bastard, you whore, you . . ."

No one ever spoke to me in this way before. I know that we plan, sometimes, the words we may use in moments of drama, and I know that the words finally used are never those we have planned—that is a commonplace. I have nothing to say to this young man now, no words to ease his suffering. I have no bandage to wipe the blood from his face. His eyes are dark now, like black grapes; he found that darkness in—North Africa, Italy? I could go to him, help him. But I, too, have my province. I am little different from the priest, the doctor, the policeman, when it is a question of determining my province. I address the man primly in my best Mind Your Shading manner.

"Mind your language young man. Kindly leave the room."

He goes, uncomforted. I start to cry the tears of a middle-aged woman; tears of drought—so few that they would nurture no growth of mourning or of comfort; they are neutral tears, drawn from the world's supply. My throat is sore, my shoulders heave. One plait falls from its carefully-pinned crown onto my breast, and I notice that once again it is golden brown as it used to be, brushed three hundred strokes a night; and I remember how I sat with my easel and paints (Wilfred bought me the canvas folding stool) near the mouth of the Waitaki, trying to paint it. I try to see it now, but I cannot. The water is blistered, the foam has changed to blood; I stamp my foot in grief and rage.

"Where's the reason for it?" I cry.

"But you were always so good at shading," my mother replies, from nowhere. "Remember how you used to be first in the class for shading!"

I stop crying now, and choosing another golden brown square to sit in, I go to sleep, and when I wake, still in the room two inches behind the eyes, my sister Lucy is standing rich, proud, vague, in the center square.

· 24 ·

I KNOW THAT IT is Lucy standing in the room, for recognition of Lucy, Roland, Graham, Fernie, does not demand any special memory of them. They simply *are,* as domestic objects or land-marks. Perhaps the clarity in which they appear now (for Roland has entered the room, with Graham and Fernie) is a sign of their obscurity in a particular memory. They have the nondescriptness that I noted in my mother. Lucy stands there, eternally rich, vague, dreamy, thinking about her native plants—alpine shrubs are in fashion this year; rock gardens, cacti are out; snow orchids (if you can find them) are in, with native plants, too, but the alpine shrubs take precedence—Lucy thinking about her tapestries, her new house, her new hobby of singing (she has entered for the Dunedin Competitions this year, The Ladies' Rose Bowl), not as ambitious as might be imagined, for she has always had a pleasant singing voice, like our father; she is thinking now of her husband, her son, our family, of how she will remain "loyal" to Matuatangi, unlike her elder sister who has deserted the town that her father helped to build. (When Lucy drives visitors around Matuatangi she behaves like a landlady, or the squire's wife showing off the estate.) She dresses neatly, she has no evident cares, she entertains, she reads the recommended books and one or two that she daringly discovers on her own.

"Have you read *Little Known Facts of the Thirteenth Century*," she will ask her guests, adding, "I came across it by chance. Take no notice of the title! It's the most fascinating book I've read for some time; extremely readable, too."

Lucy casts a spell over people who know her. A week or two later her friends and guests are absorbed in the *Little Known Facts of the Thirteenth Century*. (The town librarian cannot understand the sudden popularity of history!) Everyone is talking of thirteenth-century characters as of personal friends; Christian names are dropped, bartered; wars, knights, the results of jousts fall like recipes, like lullabies, like trotting doubles from their housewifely, League-of-Mother lips. Yet Lucy is not to be thought of as empty-headed. She *knows* people; perhaps the extent of her knowing can be summed up thus: she can bring a plumber from *nowhere* to plumb on a public holiday!

The vacant spaces in Lucy's mind that would not receive the processes of mathematics, remain vacant, and from time to time the vacancy is inclined to spread, like weed on a stagnant pond; such weed can be eliminated with method, but Lucy has little method. This is not wholly a disadvantage. When I think of her

I find that perhaps in order to cloud the issue of old conflicts and jealousies, I adopt my schoolteacher approach.

"Lucy, watch your shading!"

She could never draw. I suppose her gift is in her voice. She was always clever at reciting poetry. She used to recite from *Tarantella*,

Never more, Miranda, never more.
Only the high peak's hoar,
And Aragon a torrent at the door.

and a poem about a highwayman,

The moon was a ghostly galleon tossed upon cloudy seas

Yet, though her enunciation was good, she did not have the imagination to capture the far places.

Again, I find that when I think of her, I judge, judge, adding remarks to her school report,

"Lacks imagination."

"Lacks method."

"Mathematics poor."

"Has no sense of perspective; shading inferior."

Yet, I do remember the image of the highwayman clattering over the cobbles up to the old inn door, tapping with his whip on the shutters, then looking up to the window where Bess, "the landlord's daughter, the landlord's blackeyed daughter" plaited "a dark-red love-knot into her long black hair." Plaiting! Lucy had short hair. It was I who used to plait my hair so carefully, brushing it three hundred strokes a night; but my hair was golden brown. "Plaiting a dark-red love-knot into her long black hair." The romantic picture appealed, I suppose. Highwaymen, old soldiers home from the war—one can be diverted so easily from one's closest concerns to wander without compass or map or language into another century among other people. Highwaymen were always so capable. Old soldiers home from the war knew all the tricks, pitfalls, and pleasures of their trade; they could rescue maidens, solve riddles, ride again into the wilderness to unearth treasure; they were so responsible, so independent, so blameless, living in an era of privilege, between the clean pages of books that showed not one drop of blood or one unmanly abusive phrase.

Perhaps I envied Lucy that she was able to spend her time with these old soldiers and highwaymen while knowing the closer comfort of Roland—a nondescript man, neutral in tone—thus, with the poet's capacity receive a wider range of color than a man whose distinction, brilliant in itself, repelled brilliance from another source; Roland, with a poet's capacity, but not a poet's knowledge of engineering; skill is needed to attract and channel the overflowing brilliance from beyond oneself, an act that comes naturally to the seasons, gray clouds soaking the sunlight, those flowering cherry trees that draw the color, like wine, from the cask of sun. Roland just did not and does not have the filtering process, the engineering technique to light his gray self with splendor. Lucy has the secret formula and uses it.

Graham, too, has a share. Whatever feeling I had for Graham is buried now. When the decision was made for me to care for Mother, it was not my decision alone. I do not mean that Lucy and Graham influenced me, or that Mother decided, or that I decided on my own. In every family there develops an operating logic with rules drawn partly from mythical families, religious edicts, and social example. It is always difficult to challenge this logic. It is sacred; few dare challenge it. Its working can be seen in the various "rules" that begin beyond history, with fairy tales. It is the youngest or eldest son who goes to seek his fortune. The eldest goes with gifts, money; the youngest goes penniless, in rags. It is the middle son who must bear his ordinariness, clumsiness, side by side with the handsomeness of his elder, the charm of his younger brother. So many of these rules still apply! The eldest son going to service in India; the black sheep of the family taking an immigrant ship to the colonies; here, the eldest son taking over the farm.

But here, there and everywhere, the unmarried eldest daughter cares for the aging parents. My role in this modern myth was not even decided by words. Someone said, one evening, "There's Mother, of course."

We looked at each other, thinking, Yes, of course, there's Mother. Then Lucy (it was a family party) turned to Roland, and perhaps no one else noticed it, but I saw her draw closer to him. Then Fernie came up to Graham and took his hand. It was like one of those party games of choosing. I was left alone, feeling my aloneness, and then, quite suddenly, the decision was made, the matter arranged, when Lucy with a neat sense of drama looked at me (all in the room were now looking at me) and repeated, "There's Mother, of course."

How I hated this wordless family communication. It is dictatorship, it is judgment without jury or appeal. And though there had been no word spoken about my being cast in the role of Mother's nurse, when Lucy was leaving (oh, those front-door remarks!), "I'll come in from time to time in the afternoon to look after her, so you needn't feel completely *tied.*"

It is not that I objected to looking after Mother. I felt I was in distinguished historical company! But an invalid is a whole world, sheets are sky and cloud, lanolin is swamp, face and body are quarter-acre sections that mustn't be abandoned, that must be tended always, plot, lawn, buildings—the seasonal show for the neighbors or for the Horticultural Society.

I objected to the restrictions put upon my view. Bed, bed mat, bed pan, bed table; the quarter-acre circumference of sickness; the mask of roses that disguised the smell of sickness. I did not know that my mother cared so much for the sun shining on the autumn lilies. She never spoke of it to me. How many other thoughts did she keep secret?

What a diminished world she and I lived in! A world of small objects, too small for shading. After my mother became bedridden, she did not lie and sit or stand under the sky ever again. One would have thought that God, going about lifting the roofs of the houses, like pie crusts, would have lifted the roof of my mother's bedroom for her to have the sky directly above her. I had no idea that the sky interested her so much, or that she missed it. I have been obtuse in many ways, too generous with my own opinions, suppositions, interpretations, shading everything according to my own view, thinking it was the general view, and it may have been, I don't know, I'm sure I don't know. And now here is Graham, legal and Christchurch-looking, standing with Fernie and Lucy and Roland, displaying their ordinary nondescript essence without self-pity, for people are content, in the end, to be crushed, absorbed in others, lost under avalanches, in mines, buried forever in the earth; it's nothing to fight against, they say, it's just there and will come and that is that.

Yes, that is that.

And why should we fly with crimson wings or wear yellow roses or shine like the aquamarine underside of wild birds and tropical fish, glint with ideas, glitter with our special essence, like the gold dust on the butterflies' wings, when the earth itself is brown and dust is gray, and our flesh is lumps of dough that are swallowed without special praise or blame—oh why, in the beginning, do we not stay raw, running together, merging into one on the hot, black tray, third, fourth, first from the sun?

Now as I observe Lucy, Roland (There is an oil tanker in port. Tonight he and Lucy will go to the cocktail party on board), Fernie, Graham (he is two inches taller since he went to live in Christchurch; two inches of civic pride), I know that they are not my besiegers. What would they want from me? Why would they knock in the middle of the night in a storm, to get into my white house on the hill? Is it perhaps someone I don't know who besieges me? It may indeed be a character from a fairy tale, an old soldier home from the wars. (How my mind returns to that old soldier!)

Or is it someone I knew in Matuatangi? How far away Matuatangi seems from my subtropical paradise, my island where storms are stormier, rain is rainier, sun is sunnier, where violets bloom in winter, daffodils are withered long before springtime, flax flowers, sucked by wax-eyes and fantails, dart their curved beaks to and fro in the wind. How should I feel if I returned to Matuatangi now, if I traveled in sleep, step by step of the journey observing, observing, with my new vision that does not seem to be so new after all? I raise my hand to paint; I may end by striking; I fancy that I can wield well a paintbrush, a pencil, crayons, that I may be able to brand, as painters do, my individual vision of the world. Even as I think this I know in my bones—a dark, terrible, ineradicable place of knowing—that my eye goes towards a shadow as a hawk dives to a rabbit, that my shade-calculator leaps into action—how much black, gray, neutral tone . . .

I must remember that if I returned to Matuatangi there would be no home. The house is sold now. If only the big decisions of one's life were not so often attended by chattels—tables, beds, chairs, expecting to be carried on the airy-fairy bandwagon of the spirit! Yet, why should not wood (in its shape as furniture and books) make this demand, since, earlier, as trees, it sheltered our Gods and ourselves, and as part of the first objects springing under the sun, gave us the first shadows, shadows moving lace-woven, dancing, patterning light and shade, golden bee-striped shadows stinging the sight with their fresh view, promising honey of light and dark? We ought to be able to bear, with our spirits, the chattels we make from trees, carrying, too, a heartful of birds to sing in the glossy leaves.

So I dream and journey, with half my mind telling me that I am here at Karemoana in my white house on the hill overlooking the gulf, in a night of storm and knocking, while I walk down the winding, newly tar-sealed road to the ferry, board it, walk down the rotting staircase to the cabin, warm globuled with oil from the engine, choose my slatted seat leeward, and with my feet slapped with sea water, sway back and forth as we smoke, chuff, gurgle, chug-chug our weather-worn way out of Kare-moana into the gulf, into the harbor, into Auckland; knowing, with the dismay that all travelers feel, that this is not the end of the journey, that much waiting, jogging, many states of "passing through," from the severe state of spending one day in Wellington, in transit, to the milder form of an hour and a half waiting on the Christchurch Railway Station, must be suffered before I arrive at Matuatangi. Only in dreams could I make this journey without fatigue!

·25·

IN MY DREAM I do not arrive at Matuatangi. I do not even reach the Auckland Railway Station. I cross from Karemoana in the ferry, choose a seat on the waterfront, and sit there watching the world go by, and as I see the world going by I notice a middle-aged woman with gray hair wound in plaits, a brown costume, not in the latest fashion but bought (I suppose) four or five years ago from a Matuatangi shop where the models of the thirties are still poised, dowdily dressed, with drooping hems and shoulders. I notice the woman's shoes, brown, with open-work across the front in an arch-comfort style; the stockings that are obviously stockings and not the "bare-leg look"; the handbag, the gloves, the brooch on the bosom of the chiffon blouse. I snap my lips in

triumph—a Matuatangi woman, I exclaim, dressed for the Matuatangi climate. Here, up north, she should be wearing a summer
dress with a bolero to smarten it and hide her flabby upper arms
from the gaze of the slim young women in tight pants who think,
No, not me in fifty years' time, surely! Gray hair and flabby arms
and an extra pocket in my stomach where there's no further need
for an extra pocket to receive and feed, like a crevasse in a
concrete path or a runnel in a clay bank, the wind-blown thistle-
seed, the one o'clock of the season. Who is this woman from
Matuatangi? I wonder obtusely. How *wedded* she is to her
clothes! If she, like me, were ever overcome with the urge to
break free from her former life, to change her view, she would
never succeed. She travels her life in her clothes, using them not
as garments of modesty, fashion, convenience, but as props to
support her, each garment with its special duty not in any way
related to the physical propping that is, alas, also necessary. Who
is this woman to have let her clothes cloth-crash her spiritual life?
Tweed-wool-chiffon-swathed, mummy-wound, shrouded, preserved, pronounced dead, she will never break free. I should
go to her, introduce myself, explain that to change her view of
life in middle age is impossible because for so long she has been
married to everything about her, because her clothes cling so
tightly to her essence—when she goes home tonight and hangs up
her costume would she consider it for a moment, thinking, not
how she has left her shape in it and must iron it out, but how
much it has stolen her shape as its rightful possession? The
human body gives up its life more readily than the clothes it has
worn—the clothes of the dead embrace life as the fingernails and
hair absorb the last concentrate of the body's being. I know, from
my mother's clothes. In the end, they were night clothes only,

locknit nighties that stole the smell of her body when they could no longer find enough life to steal.

This woman from Matuatangi appears dazed. She has an intelligent face, its shape kept only because the face does not wear a garment to steal the shape. Her face, confused in its expression, looks out at the hot, high sky. It is strange that so little of the body is given such care, lavished so deeply with longing for preservation, as the face receives. Day after day, year after year, we go in our lives face to face, face to face, searching, reading, scanning, interpreting, translating in our own language what we have discovered in the face thrust close to us, with its lips and tongue and throat working in speech, its eyes traveling (eyes *do* travel, "down to Oxford towers") from destination to destination. As long as one has sight, one need never travel in train, car, plane or boat. The eye is the most enduring, fashionable, thorough tourist, especially when it makes these tours of faces that bob before it, like peninsulas of flesh surrounded by seas of air, coasting down to the mysterious mainland that is swathed in its *clothes.*

Now the woman from Matuatangi has gone, out the wharf gates into Lower Queen Street, down among the fish-and-chip and oyster bars and the tobacconists selling their Giant Kiwi tickets, First Prize Sixty Thousand Pounds, among the overflowing dust bins, the fruit shops, the smart, new, sandwich-and-milk bar, cool as a temple, with its confession boxes side by side along the wall, head high.

I don't know where the woman from Matuatangi has gone now, lost in the heat and the clouds of white hats and gloves that float like summer parachutes up and down the street.

I sit here alone, watching the pigeons, putting an intensity into watching them, as if their every movement had more significance than it has in fact—this, people do when they sit alone in concentrated gazing. On the other seat on the edge of the wharf there is a middle-aged man staring with the same kind of concentration at the pigeons. He has the expression of someone watching a football match. An involuntary jerk of his head, of his hand, expresses delight, concern, appreciation of a fat, mess-bespattered pigeon waddling from here to there, of a struggle between two pigeons for a banana skin, or of a lone pigeon's one-foot stand, rocked with the light breeze, on the very edge of the wharf.

"Will he fall? Will he be blown into the water?"

(He's on the touch-line now. Will he score?)

The overseas ships, incontinent as ever, keep up their rush of water into the sea. Workmen treading sea-weathered planks suspended from the deck paint the rusted hull in preparation for the next journey. A crane, creaking, hangs, leans down to grasp discovered treasure from the dark hold.

Each movement of each object is noted intensely by the man. I watch, too, trying not to let myself be drawn into what is not a drama and has none of the elements of drama; no, indeed (I say primly), to let myself become involved with the affairs of pigeons, of cranes, of workmen balancing on rotten planks to paint a rusty ship. I have chosen as *my* involvement, the scenery, the *natural scenery* of my country.

Yet—the man on the plank may fall; he sways dangerously. This gust of wind may blow that impertinent sea gull from his perch on the edge of the wharf. This down-and-out, old-age pensioner, I suppose—his clothes are shabby, slept-in, his face is covered with stubble, his two nostrils are nipped at the edges, like pastry, and have the color of pastry, his hands that clench, unclench, as he follows the scenes and acts of his wharf drama, are wormed with veins. His shoes are down at heel. He has the responsible, leisurely air of one who is trying to fill in time, as if time were a grave. I have the impression when he leans suddenly forward, his head jerked to one side, empathetically imitating one of the sea gulls—though his expression is not that seen in the glitter-bright gulls' faces—that he is like a man who leans over a grave and sees the satined and coffined dead torn suddenly from respectability.

Now the hobo, vagrant, call him what you will (he has no doubt spent the morning wandering the streets), picks up a discarded cigarette butt and without a grimace, puts it in his mouth, while I, sitting here so neat, so particular always in my dress and habits, feel a desire to vomit. Where has all our training in public hygiene led us if these nasty old men persist in picking up and smoking cigarette butts? My indignation and disgust have quite overcome my resolve to avoid the pseudo-drama of pigeons and sailors precarious on planks. Why, the thought of "sailors precarious on planks" has the same unreal air, like

Little birds are playing bagpipes on the shore

or,

Little birds are choking baronets with bun,
Thanks they cry 'tis thrilling,
Take, O take this shilling.

I almost expect to see dead baronets. I find that my concern with them is not so much with their choking as with the fact that the baronets should have so little knowledge or care about hygiene that they *accept pieces of stale* bun from the dirty little birds! It is the concern of the birds and not of myself that, for so long, the birds have been willing to accept, be choked by, buns from baronets!

The vagrant on the seat (we do not call them beggars now; by not calling them beggars we think we have abolished beggars) stands up, takes a piece of torn newspaper from his pocket (goodness knows what week or year it is. How virtuous one is, I feel, if one has *today's paper* in one's pocket, if one has got rid of all yesterday's and the day before's unsavory news); still smoking the cigarette butt that clings to his lips and is sucked rather than smoked, the vagrant walks towards me, his gait leisurely, suited to one who is filling in time. I notice on the lapel of his coat a small badge—an R.S.A. badge! So this is the old soldier home from the wars—does not the R mean "returned?"—the man who used to charm princesses from sleep, who could dance all night in an underground palace, row home across an underground stream, and not suffer the twinges of an old man's rheumatism; who could slay dragons, go in search of and find buried treasure, share his last slice of bread and butter with the sick fox who could not (he thought wrongly) hope to reward him; who willingly carried the wood for the woodcutter's wife, not knowing that his burden would change to diamonds. There's some mistake, some mistake, I think, and I shut my eyes, blotting the dream from the dream; and then, suddenly, this old soldier home from the wars begins to work his mouth like the preparation of guns to fire a volley, and in a swift movement he thrusts his head forward, jetting his butt, globed with spit, to the ground at my feet.

I wish then that the woman from Matuatangi would come back to stand beside me as an ally against this shocking lack of education in hygiene, old soldier home from the wars or not. My former self as a schoolteacher rises in me, as a drowned body rises in full view of the world where it will be rescued—or salvaged, with public interest and inquiry, or will drift unnoticed downstream to the sea and be submerged forever.

I wait, sitting on the wharf seat, for the woman from Matuatangi to return. How comfortable, how correct, well-chosen, I think to myself, was her brown costume. How erect she held herself; a spine like a rod. A woman of discipline. If she were a teacher of Art or an artist, she would be so careful with her shading. No fire shovel would go down to Hell without its attendant shadow in full glory of ebony. How I wish the woman would come back, with her plaits wound in their shining crown about her head, with her sensible shoes, her flower brooch; I remember now that the brown of her costume was not the usual unimaginative brown; its tone was subtle, that of autumn leaves when they have lost the admiring attention of people whose lives are spent looking forward to "the leaves this year" and remembering "the leaves last year" when drab, with few threads of gold left, they can go about the unheroic business of dying, of mingling with the dark brown of the earth.

Now the old soldier has gone. The sea gull has been blown over by a sudden gust; he staggers, surprised. Good, I think. Serves him right! Then I withdraw from my momentary involvement. There are no people on the wharf now. The painters have gone away; the crane hangs immobile; one by one, the sea gulls fly away; the few sailors on board go down below deck. The sun disappears behind a cloud, bringing a threat of everlasting cold. A damp sweat of dew covers the ground, the wooden seats. Mist rises from the sea to meet the mist from the sky. All is shadowy, now. I shiver. My stockings feel damp. I glance down at my shoes and note, with surprise, that they are "sensible" shoes, brown, with open-work pattern in an arch-comfort style. I look at my brown costume, rush my hand to my bosom to finger the brooch on my chiffon blouse that feels misty, damp, like a watermeadow, and the brooch is shut fast upon it like a flower gate. I touch my plaits, wound close to my head. They are smooth and shining. How strange, I think. Am I the woman from Matuatangi, imprisoned in my clothes? But where has the woman from Matuatangi gone?

Once again the rhyme comes into my head,

Little birds are playing
bagpipes on the shore
near the waters' roar.

Where have the sea gulls gone? Where are the baronets? Is it the sea gulls or the baronets who are choked, in the end? Was the old soldier home from the wars a baronet? Wilfred had a relation, a baronet, in England. He talked of him when we were comparing ancestors and firsts and who traveled or didn't travel in the earliest ships. We did not care, not really, but we had to *know.* We exchanged these arrows of prestige in the hope of gaining entry to unknown parts of ourselves. Wilfred's baronet lived in Kensington among the white houses and the clean, aristocratic, leaf-filtered light, and no doubt the trees there were filled with clean, aristocratic birds.

Not like these pigeons, choking baronets with bun, and then—why, all the little birds in the trees, in *my trees,* in my father's native trees that grew beside my rivers—Waitaki, Raggitata, Rakaia, Taeri, Kakanui, Maheno—I will say them as I say the mountains in their imprisoning chains: all the birds and baronets and the buns—Easter buns—and the South Island bagpipes, the wind rocking heel and toe on the window pane, cock o' the south skirling daylight in.

Little birds are playing bagpipes on the shore?

The trees, the birds, the mountains, the rivers and I, Malfred Signal, locked in my clothes sitting alone on the Auckland wharf waiting for the ferry to take me back to Karemoana, to the night, the storm, the knocking, waiting for daylight to come, when I shall open my front door upon a New View of the world, when I shall be faithful to myself and not to my shadow.

Thinking of my shadow, I look down at my body and I realize, with a shock of horror, that I have no shadow. Surely all objects have shadows, even in this faint light? Those dreamed may be shadowless, but surely not the dreamer? Was it perhaps my shadow, in the form of the woman from Matuatangi, who walked by me? Has my shadow shrunk, changed to a sea gull and flown away or has it been choked by baronets with bun? Baronets. Wilfred's relation. I feel now that I hate Wildred. How dare he, how dare he! Old soldier home from the wars indeed, with his lack of hygiene, picking up cigarette butts, living like a layabout in the northern city, spitting his returned overseas germs on the shining Auckland wharf!

I am tired. Forgetting my condemnation of Wilfred and his habits, my disappointment that old soldiers home from the wars are not as I dreamed them to be, my disappointment with myself for knowing that dreams are illusions, and hoping they are not so, I lie down on the slatted wooden seat, on the damp and the sea gull-droppings (Chinese White mixed with Ivory Black), staining my smart brown costume, yet not caring any more; and I sleep, and when I awake I have returned to Karemoana to my white house on the hill, with the wet, weather-sagged basket chair in the front porch, the lemon tree surrounded by the golden grass, the sighing fir tree shedding its wigwam needles with every gust of sind—wigwams, or tiny sticks, arranged with a fire burning beneath them. I am lying in bed. It is night, there is a storm, someone knocks at my door, someone wanting to get in at all costs.

I spread my mountain scenery, my rivers, my chosen canvas about me, and close my eyes, but I do not sleep. Hush-hush-hush, the grass and the wind and the fir and the sea are saying; hush-hush-hush, the graves of the sailors, of the soldiers home from the war, of the baronets, of the little birds, of farmers, of sheep, of shadows; hush-sh-sh, the bagpipes on the shore, the ocean's roar . . .

·26·

THE DREAMS I HAVE dreamed, Malfred said to herself as, waking, she looked at the time on her luminous watch. Only half past two! She repeated the time aloud, "Half past two!" tripping over it, as if it were a barbed-wire entanglement keeping enemies out or in, for was not half past two the magical hour when death, if it were coming at all during the night, seized a momentary lapse of the nightwatchman of the soul, to steal in and take possession? Was not half past two the deadly hour? The dark complement of the siesta, the early afternoon tea, when baronets, choked with sleep and buns would, in the night, be choked by some agent whose action was more sinister and permanent? No back-slapping here to bring up the fragments of swallowed death!

Malfred lay cool, with some of the suggested chill of the time entering her bones. She wondered if daylight would ever come again. She tried to remember the sight of Karemoana with the sun shining; her images were lost, they moved beyond the boundary of her mind, and though she experienced the toppling sensation of reaching for them across a surrounding edge of darkness, they were too far away for her to see clearly. They mocked, like children, flesh of one's flesh, who refuse to come when they are called.

Then, with a natural feeling of security and possession, she decided to return to the room two inches behind the eyes where she felt she might find the answer; at least she would feel at home there, the room belonged to her; had she not spent so much of her time dreaming there, especially since her mother died and left enough space, even though the hollow where her life had been uprooted remained desolate, with nothing growing there now, not even noxious weeds like deadly nightshade with its beautiful purple lanterns, or buttercups and gorse with their yellow shadows.

Confidently, she turned the door handle of the dream-room. Now that was strange! The door would not open. Her eyes closed, she thought (trying to get in, forgetting the outside world and the storm), I'll pick the lock. I'm not a practiced burglar but my mind has its instruments as burglars have their jemmies, slits of celluloid, hundreds of keys dangling from the huge rusty ring, the giant's bangle.

She concentrated; dreaming, prizing, pushing, inserting a thin inflammable wedge of blackmail (if no one dreamed you, you would die; you have no shadow) around the obstinate lock. I suppose the floor will be golden and brown squares as it used to be, she thought, putting her dream where sense and awareness decided it should be—years backward in time; I suppose the people I knew will be there—my family, Wilfred, as young soldier or old soldier; and Matuatangi, the streets, the old stone buildings, hitching posts, the Old Mill; and the rivers—ah, if I cannot get in I will charm the Waitaki to flood through this room, I will say in the vernacular of Matuatangi, of the fishermen who used to watch me sketching and painting at Waitaki's mouth, a special charm—how shall it go?

Waitaki, Waitaki,
Come down dirty,
Flood my room,
Sweep it to the river's mouth,
Grind its walls on the stones
Change the golden brown squares to pebbles,
Waitaki, Waitaki,
River that I loved and painted,
River that I walked beside,
Where I sat under the willows,
Shifted the white stones with my feet,
Come down dirty, come down dirty,
Drown the room that will not let me in.

Even as she repeated her charm she knew it would not help, that even the Waitaki did not belong so completely to her that it could set aside time and space and season to do what she asked; it was a mountain river; it had commitments as well as any human being—hydroelectric installations to keep going, snow to receive and shift, fish to house, an ocean to flow to, willows to flatter with mirrors and uproot in storms, cattle and sheep to trap, men to drown; it was involved in *being;* there would never be any time for the river that she had given her heart to, more than she had ever given her heart to man or woman, to perform special favors for her. It was all very well to love the scene of one's country if, loving it, one accepted that first stark fact and condition of loving; one must expect nothing; loses weeps, loses keeps, finds weeps, finds keeps; it was a matter of luck how one's private permutations arranged themselves.

Although the struggle with the lock seemed to have taken over an hour, Malfred found that when she looked again at her watch it showed only a quarter to three—surely, now, the time for the hand of daylight on the shoulder and the eyelid? Then suddenly there was a groaning sound, a small explosion like a penny rocket misfiring, and the door to the dream-room burst open. She stood holding the opened door, her eyes shut while she prepared herself for seeing, awake, where she had lived during her sleeping dreams. Slowly, she opened her eyes.

She was in the broom cupboard at the bottom of the stairs in her old Matuatangi home, facing, ranged against the wall, the yard broom, the soft broom, the hearth broom, the flue brushes, the stove brushes, all casting their long shadows in the suddenly glaring light. Beneath the brooms were ranged the cleaning things—polish, dusters, small brooms, scrubbing brushes, black lead, window cleaner, all the materials for attacking dust that came like sand blowing across the desert to lie in every house, and if it were left to lie, to bury the house and those who lived in it. Malfred gave an excited cry—a cry of fear—when she noticed in one corner the brass fire tongs and the old fire shovel leaning against the wall casting its special magnificent shadow unseen, unknown, as beautiful, Malfred thought, even now, as any lonely flower in the desert.

Recovering from the shock of the changed nature of her dream-room she had the presence of mind and the sense of humor to realize that a broom cupboard was on a slightly higher plane than a wood shed which, if truth were known, so many people inhabited. Her heart filled with warmth when she looked again at the fire shovel. She could have piled it, rewarding it, with all the burning coals it desired, to fill and bank all the fires in the world that it served; she could have fed it from her own heart, so dark and warm it shone, with a perfection of shadow that no drawing could ever match. She bent towards it, to touch it; what did any of the squalor of the broom cupboard matter if it contained the fire shovel that had stayed with her through so many years of her life? The brooms need never be used; some were going bald; others were going gray; they could lie there with the polishers and the cleaners and the stain removers that would remove no more stains; and the polish would cake in its tin, and crack, and grass would grow up between the cracks, and outside the dust would gather, a little at first, scarcely noticeable, then it would pile higher, gradually, making the world a desert world, annihilating sound, while those who remained alive would try to walk and make no sound in their walking; the world would be muffled, wound in a fate deadlier than if it suffered a snowfall; a choking world, a final nothingness that made real the playful fantasies of little birds and their baronets and the buns fed by the shore, the crimes in the carpetbags, all the tourist excursions into nonsense cut off, the route of their return stopped; the sky in the strange land lit with coals from a fire shovel fed with a human heart, and the night in the strange land its perfect black shadow.

Malfred felt a sudden pain over her heart. Her face went pale;

she could feel the blood going elsewhere, like people making for the door when an alarm bell rings. "My blood, unlike people, can't get out," she said to herself. "It will find there's no exit from me now." She had closed her eyes with the shock of the pain and when she opened them and reached for the fire shovel, it changed to a garden shovel, and there was the dirty old man who had been sitting on the wharf, the old soldier, filling in the grave; filling and spitting; sucking on his cigarette butt; his out-of-date newspaper poking out of his pocket.

Then the wind outside began to moan more loudly, and above its moaning and the answering moan of the sea, Malfred heard the fist-sounds on the back door. The knocking had started again.

·27·

SOMEWHERE, HIGH IN THE sky, she thought, daylight will begin, as it had always begun. If I draw aside my curtain now I will see this lightening, the shapes coming back into everything, green trees and shrubs being green again, yellow flowers yellow, the mangrove leaves gray-hearted with dust; there will be no quarreling over shape and color; each will take what belongs to it. If I did not know or surmise more about the effects of light, I should say it was an instrument of peace; almost, the generosity of morning makes me believe this. The handout is unstinted, leisurely, calm; there is no rush, panic or stampede among the natural objects for the restoration of their shape and color; they receive it in good time. Entering night, as one enters an Art gallery, they (and we) surrender everything that may be hostile to what lies within: they, their shapes and flauntings of color; we, our stabbing-sticks called umbrellas and prejudice. If I were to pull aside the curtain now . . .

The knocking sound again. There was a rush of footsteps from the front door to the back, from the back to the front door. There was no attempt this time to turn off the light. Should I open the door? Malfred began again to wonder. Should I try phoning again—the priest, the doctor, the Constable, all who are determined to stay out of the province where I find myself this evening—but what province is it, what name shall I give to it? A woman of my age can't be expected to cope for long with such a night of strangeness. There must be someone within whose province I, and whoever knocks at my door, must be welcomed. Who decides the provinces? (Ah, I know that the Waitaki decides its province, lying there in its self-assurance between Otago and Canterbury, defying each province to take arms against the other, to cross the bridge with warriors—it would not be unknown, war breaking out between province and province; but Waitaki knows its place, even when handled, mishandled, directed, misdirected by men.)

She saw the hand of her watch jerk itself towards three o'clock. The hand did not move a minute at a time, as if it had not the courage to grasp separate minutes, but every four minutes—the time allowed for warning of destruction?—it made a sudden bold, decisive leap forward. As she studied it, considering it, her mind using the words "courage," "boldness," "timidity," she reproached herself for this untidy splashing of emotion onto the objects that lay about her. She had always held the belief that objects had a right to their own being, that there need be no interpretation of them by the human mind and heart; it seemed, however, that one could not avoid spilling a little of the surplus in moments of excitement when the container overflowed and there was nowhere convenient for it to be emptied; then, as now, Malfred forgave herself the indulgence in pathetic fallacies.

Three o'clock. The time when death swings close, is gone. It is perhaps at this time that death, in its rebound, is farthest from the earth, is propelled now towards the farthest stars and planets, is scorched in its tracks by the sun; now, if ever, is the chance for daylight to put a spoke in the big wheel of night, to prepare the harlequin banners of day, to set up the feast, the gold rush; up in the sky now, the sun, first on the scene, is sitting cleaning, in its scoop of cloud, the first few grains of daylight, washing it with dew, until the dull, earthy color changes to gold. Rich day! Millionaire world!

Oh, let the sun come soon, Malfred thought. Should I charm it, she wondered, as I tried to charm the Waitaki? Why, this night, have I become so superstitious, so primitive in my mind that I have found it necessary to try to cast spells over the world, to bend it to my will?

Sun bring daylight soon to the world
Shine on Karemoana and the islands of the gulf,
Shine on my white house on the hill
With the lemon tree, the fig tree, the flax tree in the garden.
Sit in the basket chair in the front porch
Stay with us, keep night and darkness away forever.
Sun, sitting now up in the higher sky
Sifting the grains of light with dew,
Find soon the yellow light, spill it on us,
Make us millionaires of light,

Let us go walking in our gold claim up and down the world.
Sun, begin the gold rush, too soon
The world becomes a ghost town buried in poverty
The drained sky is dark
The cloud-signs hang, inviting but no light comes in.

A sudden tremendous knocking on the back door startled Malfred from her fantasies. She got out of bed, put on her dressing gown, and sat on the edge of the bed, feeling sick, looking at her rose-patterned slippers. Why was everything rose-patterned? Wallpaper, slippers, bedspread, curtains, roses growing that were roses and roses and roses? Shivering, drawing her dressing gown about her, she called out, making her decision at last,

"Who is it? If you tell me who you are, I'll open the door."

There was no answer. The knocking continued.

Malfred's shoulders drooped and she began to whimper. "Oh," she moaned softly, "who is it, who is there, who is haunting me?" Why cannot I be left in peace to live the life I have chosen to live, in communion with mountains and rivers and shrubs and valleys; rivers shallow and deep, with the sun planing the water into curled shavings of light; creeks with water waved over the white stones, blanketed with rainbows, mountain creeks cold, deep, swift; and the seas, Pacific, Tasman, tasted in their very names—Pacific, Tasman? Why cannot I be left to make my View of them, to draw from them a new intensity of vision, paint the manuka smoking with white flame, or the sky as manuka smoking with cloud; paint the shoals of light gulped down by the water; look at death, see it in the land, as I saw it in my mother's face, feel in seeing it, as I felt then; recognize it; wonder why; paint why; paint red, red, why? The glacier slides down the valley; my heart is too numb under its weight. There are some who, knowing my new purpose in painting, will remind me that I, Malfred Signal, may be regarded as a promiscuous, even an adulterous woman, to lie so with the landscape of my country, "to lie with the gaunt hills like a lover" or, like Janine, when *"Devant elle les étoiles tombaient, une à une, puis s'éteignaient parmi les pierres du désert, et à chaque fois Janine s'ouvrait un peu plus à la nuit. Elle respirait, elle oubliait le froid, le poid des êtres, la vie démente ou figée, la longue angoisse de vivre et de mourir . . . le ciel entier s'étendait au-dessus d'elle, renversée sur la terre froide. . . ."* I ask only that I be given the peace to live as I have decided to live, without my mother, father, sister, brother, lover knocking at my door; without being besieged by those who have been close to me when, in desperation to reinstate their position and claim, as people do, as long as they live and even when they die, they cunningly adopt the disguise of characters of myth and legend, they change to helpless old women or old soldiers home from the wars; not even denunciation, a ripping away of the disguise with the bandages, can uncover the deception. I want only to forget the years of rigid shading, obsessional outlining and representation of objects; I want in this, still my preliminary dream, to explore beyond the object, beyond its shadow, to the ring of fire, the corona at its circumference; I want to find whether the fire is moving, leaping alive, or whether it is petrified, a burial of past fire, stone flames whose flight and dance are illusory in that they remain fixed forever, as stone is rooted to its place of being.

Again, the knocking. I am so used to it, she thought, that in time it will tick unheard like a clock that is within time as within a shell, is within me, within the world. Knocking let me in, let me out; this insistence on being other than where one is may be the basis for the dream world, but it need not torment me in this way; me, a middle-aged, retired, Art teacher trying to lead my own life after so many years of restrictions, severing myself from my past, selling my home, taking this long uncomfortable journey north to do so; I need not be made the scapegoat for the knocking, breaking and entering, escaping, the final encircling freedom!

I wish, she thought, that I were at this moment by the Waitaki mouth, with my easel and stool and pencils and paints, all in a pleasant clutter of work, an incongruous sight on the banks of a snow-fed river; solitary fishermen, wading in salmon pools, casting their glinting spoons over the water, raking with their gaffs at the quinnat's writhing body, come up to me after they have lost or landed their fish to stare at my work.

"Painting?"

"Yes."

"A painter?"

"Yes."

The fisherman sweeps his hand in a possessive curve over the Waitaki and its surrounding country; the Southern Alps are gripped between his fingers.

"Great place to paint. Great river. Great salmon river. Or used to be."

He stands a moment watching, waiting for the miracle that doesn't happen, then, bored, he goes away, like a thirsty buffalo to his favorite water-hole.

I study the scene. I am so careful in painting to make the blue blue, the green green. I need so much to have my scenes "life-like." I paint stolidly, faithfully, until I have preserved the river on my canvas; then, satisfied, thinking of the next Art Society

Meeting when I shall offer my Waitaki paintings for exhibition, I put away my materials and leaving them by a clump of tussock or near a willow tree I walk along the river bank to the place of the stones. I am still thinking of the Art Society, the Monthly Social, Ladies a Plate, and of what I shall put on the plate, and of how I shall not be able to put the head of St. John the Baptist, or of Tom Pearce, or Tom Pearce's old mare, or of an old soldier home from the wars. I never dreamed of doing this in my unemancipated days. I study the stones, picking up those that appeal in their shape and color, pocketing some, thinking how smooth stones are, how accomplished in their being, how unhurried in their movement; stones in their lives are slow travelers with no history of passing judgment or making comparisons (the noted characteristics of travelers); still they could, if they wanted to, tell tall tales of moss, desperation in burning, murder; as plate and slate of marvel, as stone, they can be overturned where centuries and men are served, swallowed, written and learned; and skimmed on the dark water, stone may be the shadow of a cathedral.

Then with my stones and my painting materials, I walk to Waitaki bridge to catch the train to Matuatangi. I stand on the station platform. The old Railway Hotel is empty. It may soon be demolished. Part of the railway track, no longer used, disappears in a bed of thistle, wild sweet pea, ragwort, and other "railway" weeds, each displaying its supremacy from cutting to cutting throughout the land—here is the kingdom of gorse, there sow thistle, blackberry, wild sweet pea, flax, manuka. Sometimes the rule is by troika—sow thistle, dock (burned like a birthmark over the grass), sweet pea.

But what is the use of my dreaming again—I am in Kare-moana. I could not ever return to the south. I must give up forever the sight of the mountains covered with snow (I am told that one mythical snowflake fell here, one season, in Titirangi), of the clear-headed, frosty mornings and the winter chill; all the spider webs in the morning dew; the slow turning of the leaves from green to gold, not, as here, the secret changes. I must give up the nearness to ice, the sun striking with its warning chill. I must live up north until I die, up north here where I feel as if I have climbed a high ladder, an up-north ladder, with thin rungs, that I stand now high in the air that smokes with heat, ridged pawpaws drooping yellow about me, lemon trees, orange trees (the oranges are bitter), fig trees, and I am alone, in luminous metal weather, where a touch of the finger along the sky burns like the touch on hot blue steel.

And then there's the sea, a different sea, and when I think of it I try not to feel accusingly towards it; a beautiful sea, deep blue, rich, a sea of paradise such as will never flow in the south; but a different sea—oh, the human heart does not take kindly to difference!

Again, the knocking sounded. Malfred had been crouched in her dressing gown and slippers on the edge of the bed. She got up now and tiptoed to the sitting room where she switched on the light, then she went to the small bedroom in the alcove. Shall I draw the curtains? she thought again, sensing in the room the gradual leaking-in of daylight. The window does not face the sea. It does not have a row of flax bushes. Outside this window there are marigolds growing, and the ice plant, and the thin gold grass, its gold so pale that one thinks the grass may be a shadow of heavenly grass. Then, there's the path down to the gate. Who has walked along that path tonight?

She looked now like a tired woman who, unable to sleep, had got up to make herself a cup of tea, perhaps to take a sleeping pill, and on her way to the kitchen she had stopped to glance at the window; perhaps thinking, I'm safe. It's been a wild night, I must go to sleep soon.

Commonplace thoughts without anguish, simple wishes that do not bring within their boundary the past, the future, death, relations of people one with the other, love affairs with men and land, bondage with rivers. One can tell so little of another's dreams. This middle-aged woman stood there safe in her night-clothes, in her dressing gown and rose-patterned slippers, knowing that on the bench in the kitchen there was an unwashed cup, saucer and plate, that clean crockery was kept in the cupboard beside the electric range, that the cutlery had its special drawer, the cleaning materials were in the sink cupboard, the bread tin was an old biscuit tin with air holes in it to keep out the green mould . . . each detail so closely associated with one woman's way of living, serving as an anchor to bring the scene, the night, the fears, the possibilities of the continued knocking to an ordinary level of domesticity, of simplicity. Malfred Signal, the new woman in the white house on the hill couldn't sleep and was on her way to the kitchen to make herself a cup of tea.

So one would have thought. Yet always, death, the past, the future, are on guard ready to thrust meaning into the smallest gap in the simplicity; somewhere, at some time, the domestic, everyday, conventional armor wears thin.

As Malfred stared at the window there was a crash, a splintering of glass flying in all directions, onto the spare bed, onto the floor, onto the shelf by the bed, in Malfred's hair, at her feet. She stood, terrified. The wind, waiting at the window, leapt through the ragged gap, flapping wildly at the curtains; and, in a moment, the storm had entered the room, the wind was whistling through the house, all the curtains were dancing wildly. The house grew cold. When Malfred shivered, it was as much with the cold as with the shock of what had happened. The black space where the glass had been showed that daylight was still far away. A sense of collapse seemed to overcome the house, as if its walls were made of paper. While the glass had been breaking, Malfred heard beneath the crashing, the sound of the person who had broken the window—a grunt, then laughter—it was impossible to tell whether there were two people or more—then the racing footsteps of the prowler sounded in the grass and down the path and there was no more knocking.

Dazed, wondering what had broken the window, Malfred looked around the room. Beneath the window sill she saw a stone wrapped in newspaper. She picked up the newspaper and unafraid now, she walked from room to room switching on the lights. Then she spread out the paper, thinking, as she did so that it reminded her of the scrap in the pocket of the old soldier home from the wars. Scrawled across the print, in red crayon, were the words, *Help Help*. She read the news that was not in any language she had learned:

Soltrin, carmew, desse puniform wingering brime
commern in durmp, a farom a ferinwise lumner,
sturph, wolpe,
the barim in pem is striller swimmerly trone
acclime, volpone, pheme in ambertime.

Barncolum, barncolum, larnessence,
sorrowbride, merle pastime,
cloudprime
O in ambertime
in carmew fortproud hindling carmining
tench in pem strilling trone
cloudprime
ambertime
who and done,
whone, whone.
Findle with torch fiming coolth
challglace curndle perdemtory name
curge-displace kill-crime
tilth far-freedom-flame
illth, evil, torch fiming findle,
curndle, challglace
teem, fime,
torchgleam crime
cale coolth
fuming of perburning
rones, deash, done to fleath
in blame, volpone, volpone,
O in ambertime
cloudprime
who and done
whone, whone.

That was all. Help, Help, and last century's or tomorrow's
news in verse. Nothing to tell who was the writer or who had
thrown the stone.

Malfred picked up the stone. She wanted it to be a river stone
but she knew it was not. She could not name it—"lodestone, horn-
blende, amethyst, Iceland spar, hackly fracture, lustre adaman-

tine." Yet she held it fast in her hand until it seemed that it lost its chill and grew warm, with promise of sun.

Three mornings later, when they found her, both her hand and the stone held fast in her hand were ice cold; she was dead. The room, too, was cold with the sea wind. Outside, the sun, enriching the day, spilled its cleaned grains of light, and the sea lay calm at last.